THE WIDOW'S HOPE

IRIS COLE

©Copyright 2021 IRIS COLE

All Rights Reserved

License Notes

This Book is licensed for personal enjoyment only. It may not be resold. No part of this work may be reproduced in any form or by any electronic or mechanical means including information storage and retrieval systems, without written permission from the author.

Disclaimer

This story is a work of fiction, any resemblance to people is purely coincidence. All places, names, events, businesses, etc. are used in a fictional manner. All characters are from the imagination of the author.

Table of Contents

The Widow's Hope i

Disclaimer iii

Part One 1

Chapter One 2

Chapter Two 16

Chapter Three 32

Chapter Four 50

Part Two 69

Chapter Five 70

Chapter Six 82

Chapter Seven 94

Part Three 108

Chapter Eight 109

Chapter Nine 119

Chapter Ten 137

Part Four 160

Chapter Eleven 161

Chapter Twelve 173

Chapter Thirteen 187

Epilogue 213

Join Iris Coles Newsletter................................ 216

Would you like a FREE Book?......................... 216

Part One

Chapter One

Mabel Finch's arms ached, but the feeling was a familiar one.

She raised the hoe, wood splinters chafing against her callused palms, and knocked it hard against a stubborn clod. The piece of dirt shattered against the hoe's iron head, revealing the pale roots of weeds. Mabel shuffled them out of the way, working carefully around the dark green leaves of the potato plant, then banked the dark soil around the tiny mound that promised to be a big white tuber someday.

Then she moved on to the next patch, breaking out the weeds, tidying the soil. One after the other. Over and over, till the field was done.

The summer sun baked down on her bent back. It was better than cold or rain, she supposed, despite the sweat trickling beneath her bonnet. She swung the hoe again, chopped out the white roots, then banked up the soil. It happened automatically by now. Her hands did the work alone, leaving her mind free to wander.

That was seldom a good thing.

She reached the end of the row and straightened her sore back. When she turned to squint at the field, she tried to look at the dark, finished rows, not the greater part of this hilly field that was still weedy and untouched. A handful of slender figures laboured over the rows behind her; several women, a few children, some so small that they could barely lift their hoes.

"It's so hot today," said the woman nearest Mabel, brushing sweat from beneath her bonnet. "Can't we have a rest?"

Mabel glanced at the oak tree in the field's corner. Its rich green branches spread a great pool of shade that beckoned, cool and inviting, to the tired laborers. But she shook her head. "We have to finish the field today."

"Finish it!" the woman exclaimed. "I don't think it can be done."

"It has to be done," said Mabel firmly.

The woman stared at her. Anna. She'd worked side-by-side with Mabel in these fields all year, and her gaze was shrewd.

"Ned wants it done, does he?" she said.

Mabel nodded.

"If we don't do it, there's consequences for you," said Anna, her voice unjudgmental and accepting.

Mabel shrugged. She picked up the hoe and attacked the next row with alacrity. "We need to get the field done," she repeated. "For all our sakes."

"Aye," Anna muttered, joining Mabel in her work. "If Ned gets wind that this feel ain't done, you won't be the only one who suffers his wrath."

The other women caught up slowly thanks to the few moments' pause at the field's edge, and they crowded around Mabel as she worked on the potato plants. Some of the little children cried with exhaustion and the sun had not yet reached its zenith. Mabel tried not to look at them; she looked only at the potatoes, focused only on her hoe.

"He's a real beast, Ned is," said Anna with feeling.

"He's my husband," said Mabel mildly.

"More's the pity, you poor thing," said Anna.

A distant shriek caught their attention. Mabel kept working, but Anna and some of the other women straightened, watching as the huff and clatter of a steam train drew nearer. Its whistle shrieked again and goats scattered from the train tracks as the fast-moving monster bore down upon them. Mabel felt the shudder of its passing in the rich earth as it raced by, clattering and hissing, a cloud of white steam blossoming over its head.

"Look at them rich folks," said one of the women enviously.

Mabel looked up. One of the train cars had large windows, wide open to admit the summer sunshine. A row of people sat at a long table, enjoying some large meal. Men, women, and children were all dressed in finery; men with dark suits, women with silky dresses. Several looked like they were laughing. Mabel glimpsed a whole roast goose on the table before the train sped by, followed by box cars containing livestock or ordinary cargo.

She turned back to her work.

"What I wouldn't give to be as rich as them folks!" said Anna.

"Roast goose on a day that ain't Christmas? Now that would be lovely," said another woman.

"We don't even get roast goose on Christmas, never mind any other day," Anna muttered.

"I'd love those pretty dresses... or just warm dresses. And to sit around instead of working all day," the woman agreed.

"How about you, Mabel?" Anna asked. "What would you like the most if you were rich?"

Mabel paused in her work to look down at her callused hands.

"I think," she said quietly, "that when my parents both died of the pox, I was lucky not to have died with them. I think I was even luckier not to starve afterwards."

Anna's face softened. "Aye, poor lass. Ain't anybody left in the world for you, is there?"

"There's Ned," said Mabel.

"Ned's a beast," Anna repeated.

Several other women stared at her in deep shock for her audacity in calling her boss such names, but Anna didn't seem to care. She went back to hoeing. "Ned's a beast, I'm telling you. You shouldn't be grateful to him for marrying you when your parents died. More like taking advantage of you, I should think.

"He puts a roof over my head," said Mabel quietly, "and food on the table."

"Aye, but there's far more to being a husband than that," Anna grumbled.

Mabel turned back to her work, though her hands trembled a little now as she hoed the field. A roof over her head and food on the table was the only love she'd ever known from her father.

It was all the love she'd ever expect from her husband, and despite what Anna said, she *was* grateful for it.

*****

Dusk threatened on the western horizon as Mabel walked back toward the farmhouse, hurrying through the home paddock's ankle-deep grass. Her heart pounded and not only from jogging the long distance from the potato field. Her hoe bounced in her hand as she approached the barn, where no lights shone. She could only hope that Ned had thought to feed the cow, pig, and horse.

It was his duty, but that was no indication that he had actually performed it.

Lanterns burned in the old stone farmhouse whose whitewashed doors and window frames had seen better days. Mabel let herself in through the back door and tried to sound cheerful as she called out, "I'm here, darling!"

The kitchen was empty, as of course it would be; that was Mabel's domain. Ned's reply came from the sitting room. "About time," he growled.

Mabel's heart wavered. Ned sounded belligerent, as usual, but she detected no slur in his voice. For once, she believed, her husband might be sober.

She turned up the kitchen lamp and then edged into the sitting room. Ned sat in an armchair with his feet up and the paper in his hands. Its many rows of tightly crowded lettering were gibberish to Mabel.

"Would you like a cup of tea?" Mabel ventured.

Ned lowered the newspaper, revealing a face as knobbly and hairy as the potatoes he grew on his land. Lines deepened around his eyes and mouth as he frowned at her. Sprouts of greying whiskers protruded from all over his cheeks and jawline.

"No, woman," he shouted. "I would like *tea*—which should have been ready an hour ago. Where have you been?"

"We were hoeing the hill field," said Mabel demurely. She resisted the temptation to say, *Like you asked*. Ned hadn't exactly asked. He'd screamed the order at her that morning, demanding that it be done by nightfall.

"Well, what took you so long?" Ned roared. "Get to work. I want my dinner and I could do with a pot of tea!"

"Of course, darling. I'm sorry," said Mabel, inclining her head.

He buried his face in his paper again, and Mabel allowed herself a small sigh of relief as she retreated to the kitchen.

She shuttered the windows against the growing darkness, stoked the pot-bellied coal stove in the corner, and got to work. First she hung the kettle over the fire—Ned would be somewhat appeased by his pot of tea—and then she raided the little garden beside the house for carrots and turnips. She selected a fine, fat young cockerel from the coop, wrung its neck and plucked it quickly while the kettle boiled. By the time she'd finished Ned's pot of tea, the chicken was in the oven with carrots and turnips. It would feed them for two or three days, she believed, especially combined with the ample rice bubbling on the stove.

Ned only grunted when she delivered tea and promised that the food would be ready shortly. It was a small blessing; his grunt was not accompanied by cursing or a cuff to the back of the head. Instead, Mabel returned to the kitchen in peace. She swept out the little room, then took a seat at the table to drink her own tea. It was the first time she'd sat down all day.

She sipped her tea slowly, watching the flicker of light in the stove. A hint of contentment crept through her heart. She clung to it fiercely, trying not to think of the train and all the rich folks on it.

I am rich, she reminded herself. *I have everything I need.*

Yet the hollowness inside her wouldn't go away.

"Woman!" Ned thundered. "*Where* is my dinner?"

"I'm coming!" Mabel called.

She bounced to her feet and took the chicken and vegetables from the oven. Her hands trembled as she poured the juices over a mound of rice on Ned's plate just the way he liked it.

He never came into the kitchen. She tried not to think that it had something to do with Sally, the wife he'd lost two years before marrying Mabel. Maybe Sally had loved the kitchen as much as Mabel did. His absence was a painful reminder that he'd loved her better than he'd ever love Mabel, even though Sally had never been able to have children. Mabel had never seen him shout at Sally in the marketplace the way he shouted at her.

She hastened to the dining table in the sitting room and set Ned's plate in order. He stomped to his chair and threw himself down in it, then tucked his napkin into his shirt.

"Chicken's underdone," he growled.

Mabel swallowed. "I could—"

"Sit and eat, woman," Ned barked. "My patience with you is spent."

"Yes, dear," said Mabel demurely.

She swallowed her tears as she returned to the kitchen for her own plate, thinking of what Anna had said. *There's far more to being a husband than that.* Anna's husband was a poor cobbler, but he always smiled when he came to walk Anna home from the farm.

Mabel pushed the thought aside as she brought her plate to the table and sat. She gazed down at the hearty meal; the chicken wing, the pile of vegetables, the heap of brown rice.

"What are you just staring at your food for? Eat!" Ned demanded.

Mabel ducked her head. "Yes, dear," she murmured, and bit into a forkful of hot, wholesome food.

Anna was wrong. Ned provided her with this, something better than she'd had even when her parents were still alive. He did everything a husband should.

She had to cling to that belief. It was the only thing holding back the tide of misery always threatening in the back of her mind.

*****

Mabel sat very quietly on the front seat of the wagon. It creaked and rumbled down the bridleway between the fields, their horse plodding along patiently, his blinkered head swinging side to side as though taking in the summer's day.

It was a lovely day, warm and sunny, and Mabel was grateful she didn't have to walk down to the barley field today. Ned didn't trust her with the horse and equipment. Instead, she swayed along with the wagon's gentle movement, grateful for the chance to rest her feet.

"Look at these fields," Ned muttered.

Mabel obediently raised her head and gazed at the fields on either side of her. Potatoes grew on the hill, barley in the lower fields. The rich green clumps of potatoes looked darker than ever compared with the paler green of the barley fields beyond.

"They're beautiful," she said.

"Are you stupid, woman?" Ned thundered.

Mabel flinched. "N-no."

"*Look* at these fields! There's nothing beautiful about them!" Ned yelled. "They're wilting in this drought. We need rain. *Now!*"

He shouted the word at her as though expecting her to magically produce the moisture the crops needed. Mabel hung her head.

"As if it's not bad enough being a farmer in this day and age," Ned muttered.

"The potatoes look well," Mabel hazarded.

Ned scoffed. "And the barley? I don't suppose you've been paying any attention to the barley, have you, woman? You know that's where our living comes from!"

Mabel swallowed. "We... we've spent the past two weeks on the potato fields, dear."

"Neglecting the barley, of course." Ned snorted. "I thought as much."

You could have come down to look at the fields yourself, Mabel thought. Of course, she didn't say it.

Her body quivered as the wagon rocked nearer to the barley fields. Ned didn't glance at the potatoes, which were almost ready for harvest. Instead, he glowered at the far larger fields of grain that took up most of the farm.

He yanked the horse to a halt. The animal tossed its head in protest, then cowered when Ned leaped down from the wagon. Mabel hovered on the seat, unsure what her husband wanted.

"Well?" Ned barked. "Are you coming or not?"

"I'm right behind you, dear." Mabel scrambled down and jogged to catch up with him.

Ned stumped to the field's gate, his boots heavy and ungainly. Mabel wondered if he'd been at the bottle, then dismissed the thought. No, surely not. They'd come straight to check on the fields after the Sunday church service. He wouldn't have... would he?

She stayed close behind him as he marched through the gate and into the field. The waist-deep crop stirred in the soft breeze, thick and grassy-looking. Ned grabbed a fistful of the nearest plant and wrenched leaves and heads from it.

"No, no, no," he growled. "By Jove! No!"

"Wh-what's wrong, dear?" Mabel ventured.

"Can't you see, woman?" Ned roared. "Look at this crop. Look at it!"

He crushed a head of barley in his meaty hands and held them out to Mabel. Her heart skipped as she stared at the grains on his palm. The crop was already drying—the edges of the head were yellow—but the grains were half the size they should be.

"Curse this drought," Ned roared. He shook a fist at the sky. "Where's the rain? We need rain!"

Mabel stared at the barley fields, her heart pounding. She had no head for numbers—no one had ever taught her arithmetic—but she knew the glaring facts. Ned had borrowed money from the bank to buy barley seed for these fields.

If this harvest failed, he wouldn't be able to pay it back. And then what?

Her hands were shaking already, and they shook far more when Ned rounded on her. "This is your doing," he hissed.

She stared at him, helpless horror spreading through her chest. "*My* doing?"

"Don't talk back to me!" Ned thundered.

Mabel cowered. "I'm sorry, dear. I just don't understand."

"How could you not understand? I just told you that you've been neglecting the barley in favour of the potatoes. The barley is the reason we're in debt!" Ned roared. "You should have taken better care of these fields!"

It would have made no difference. These fields needed rain, not attention. But Mabel dared not mention that. She simply hung her head in shame and nodded, agreeing with her husband's every word. "I'm sorry, dear."

"I should hope you are," Ned hissed. "If this crop fails, we're ruined. Do you hear me? Ruined!" He shook a fist under her nose. "It'll be your fault."

A huff of his breath washed over her face, and Mabel held back a gasp of shock. He *had* been drinking. Had she sat beside a drunkard in church that morning?

"Get back to the wagon," Ned snarled.

Mabel ducked her head and complied as quickly as she could, struggling to hold back the heavy knot of tears in her throat.

Maybe Anna is right. Mabel shoved the thought away as she scrambled onto the wagon.

Ned hefted himself up behind her, wrenched the horse's head around and whipped the helpless animal into a trot.

She tried not to think about Anna's opinions of what a husband should and shouldn't be. Instead, she allowed Ned's words to run through her mind again.

If this crop fails, we're ruined.

What did that mean? How bleak was their future really?

Chapter Two

Weeks rolled past, and no rain fell.

The barley shrivelled in the fields as Mabel watched. She tried to show Ned that she was paying attention. She brought him the sad, blighted heads even though he always screamed at her when she did so. She checked the walls and fences around the fields to keep hungry neighbouring livestock out. She walked through the fields for hours each day, bringing the other women with her, searching out every weed that might steal precious water from the crop. Each time she pulled a weed from the earth, the dirt clung to its roots in dry clods.

But no human effort could save the crop. It needed rain, and day after day, week after week, the pitiless blue sky glared down on the farm, bringing forth not a drop.

The sun poured richly over the village one Saturday several weeks later, making sweat run down the small of Mabel's back. She ignored it in favour of waving a long birch switch at the shrinking backsides of the herd of pigs in the lane in front of her.

"Go on!" she yelled, waving the switch. "Go on!"

Confused, the pigs hesitated as they approached the market square of the little village. They'd grown up in the farm's pasture; they'd never walked on cobblestones.

"Go on," Mabel sang out, swishing the stick from side to side to make a noise.

The pigs lowered their twitching muzzles to the stones, small eyes shifting suspiciously.

"Get up!" Ned roared.

He slapped his switch sharply across the buttocks of the old black-and-white boar. The animal roared at the indignity and scrambled forward, and the herd followed, heading toward the market pens surrounding the square. Several farmers had already set up stands to sell their vegetables, cheese, and eggs. Livestock lowed, filling the marketplace with sound.

Mabel hurried to stop a young sow from breaking away from the herd. She flicked the sow's ear with the switch, and the animal veered away, then darted into a pen. Ned swung the gate shut behind her. Only the old boar remained outside; he'd be sold separately.

"You'll be fine with him," Ned grunted.

Mabel raised her head and stared at her husband. Sweat trickled over his red face, but his eyes were too rheumy even for the hot day. "You—you want me to put him up on my own?"

"That's what I said, woman. Drat. Listen to me!" Ned barked.

He turned and walked away, moving faster than he ever did on the farm. Mabel was unsurprised that he chose to head directly toward the inn.

She looked away and faced the boar instead. The large animal's hide bristled with long hair. He kept his head low, belligerent grunts escaping him.

"Come on, old fellow," Mabel murmured. "In you go."

She touched him lightly with the switch. Aggravated by Ned's harshness, the boar whirled to face her with a loud squeal. Mabel jumped back out of range of the animal's thick tusks.

"Come on, come on," she whispered, waving her switch. "Go inside."

The boar's hackles rose. He backed away from her, squealing deep in his chest, and his haunches rammed into a table stacked with beets and turnips.

"Hey!" The farmer steadied his table. "Control your pig!"

"Sorry, sir. I'm so sorry," Mabel whispered.

Tears gathered at the corners of her eyes. Ned had promised that this year's batch of piglets could pay for repainting the house, which was in dire need of attention. Instead, he'd sold the entire herd because of the drought. Mabel didn't know if it would be enough to save the farm with the barley dying in the fields.

She struggled with her tears and focused on the pig. "This way, old fellow," she croaked. "Get on!"

She waved the switch, and the pig lunged. He snatched the switch out of her hands with his jaws and shook it, bellowing with rage. Mabel's heart skipped with terror.

"Here!" someone cried.

Mabel glanced up. She barely noticed the person speaking to her—a young man in a suit—and focused instead on the edge of the wooden board he held out to her.

"Grab it!" he said.

Mabel didn't need telling twice. She seized the board, and together, she and the stranger approached the boar. Faced with a solid surface, the boar backed away. He still grumbled, but made no attempt to charge them as he shuffled slowly backward and into the sale pen.

Mabel crashed the gate shut and leaned on it, breathing heavily. Beside her, the stranger tied it with string.

"There!" he said, with a gentle laugh. "Safely inside."

"Thank you," said Mabel, looking up at him for the first time.

To her surprise, the man who'd helped her looked like a gentleman. He wore a thick black suit with a waistcoat and the bright chain of a pocket watch shimmering in the sun. Rectangular eyeglasses made his brown eyes seem bigger. Soft black hair fell in raven sweeps over his forehead, and he had straight teeth when he smiled, creasing the corners of his eyes.

"Th-thank you," Mabel repeated.

"Of course. You were brave to try to get him in there on your own." The young man laughed. "I wouldn't have had the courage."

Mabel blinked, trying to find the undercurrent of meanness in his words, but there was none. It seemed that this well-dressed young man had offered her a real compliment.

The thought made her blush as a bolt of warmth rushed through her. "Thank you," she repeated.

The young man tilted his head to the side, smiling. "I take it you do have more words than that in your vocabulary."

Vocabulary? Mabel didn't know what that was, but she got the gist of what he was saying, and the gentle joke made her laugh. "I can also say, 'I'm pleased you helped me.'"

The young man grinned. "I'm Percy Mitchell."

"Mabel Finch. It's nice to meet you," said Mabel. "Wait, Percy Mitchell? Aren't you the new lawyer who's come to our town?"

"That's right," said Percy, "so if your father or brother ever needs a will or a representative in court, you know who to ask."

Mabel laughed softly. She couldn't remember the last time she'd laughed; it felt good. "That's nice to know, Mr. Mitchell."

"*Mabel!*"

Mabel's body tensed, the warmth dropping instantly from her chest. She raised her head as Ned stormed from the inn, his eyes murderous.

"Who's that?" Percy asked.

Mabel's heart clenched. "My husband," she said.

Percy looked in shock from Ned's greying head to Mabel's youthful features, then backed away. "It was nice meeting you."

"Thanks for the help," Mabel whimpered.

"Mabel!" Ned roared. "Come. We're going home."

"But the pigs," Mabel cried.

"They've been sold." Ned waved a leather pouch that clinked with money. "That fool Vernon from the south side bought them for much more than they're worth. Come on. We have to go before he realizes."

Percy's eyebrows rose, and shame pooled in Mabel's gut.

"Ned, dear—" she began.

Ned grabbed her arm. "Come," he growled. "Let's go."

Mabel had no choice but to follow him as he strode out of the market square. She glanced over her shoulder as she was dragged away and saw Percy still standing by the boar's pen, hands in his pockets, head tilted to one side as he watched her go.

*****

Manure stained the front of Mabel's dress. Its rich stench rose in her nostrils as she pitched another forkful onto the wheelbarrow outside the barn, then turned back to the dirty stall.

"Sorry," she muttered to the horse that grazed in the paddock outside the barn, his coat still marked with sweat from the wagon's harness. It had been days since she'd had time to muck out his stall.

Trying to save the barley crop took everything she had.

Mabel thrust the fork beneath a heap of manure and flicked it onto the wheelbarrow. Her hands stung with blisters as sweat ran over her palms. The pitiless sun glared down on the farm, but she knew it was cooler than before. Harvest time was coming.

And still every ear of barley remained thin and hopeless as the crop drooped in the fields.

What would happen if the crop wasn't good enough for them to feed themselves? Would they have to sell the farm? Where would they live?

Worry swirled at Mabel's feet like a vortex ready to suck her in and drown her. She tried to ignore it and flung another forkful of manure onto the wheelbarrow.

A clatter of hooves grasped her attention. Mabel looked at the horse first, thinking he'd escaped, but he stood in his paddock with his head held high. He whinnied.

Horses and a carriage, Mabel realized. They were coming down the lane—and this was the only farm on the road.

Few people ever visited here, even fewer who drove a pair, and Mabel instantly knew who it was. She ignored the dismay that weighed down her limbs and threw down the pitchfork, then sprinted to the house.

"Mabel!" Ned thundered from the sitting room. "*Mabel!*"

"I'm here!" Mabel called. She rushed through the kitchen, pulling off her filthy apron as she went. "I'm coming!"

"Ada and Alf are on their way," Ned barked. "They've just turned down the lane. Did you know about this?"

Mabel stared up at him helplessly. His bloodshot eyes were belligerent, his hands curled into loose fists by his side. The smell of stale beer drifted on his breath.

"No," she whispered. "How was I to know, dear?"

Ned sneered and raised a hand as though to strike her. He never had, but she hastened back a few steps anyway.

"Don't use that tone on me, woman," he barked. "Look at you! Get decent! Now!"

Mabel ducked her head and fled. She raced to the kitchen first to hang the kettle over the fire, then to their bedroom, a place she dreaded and avoided as much as she possibly could. She pulled her only other dress from the wardrobe: navy with a starched collar. Only her Sunday best would do for Ned's sister, Ada, and her husband.

Mabel dressed as quickly as she could, pulling her own corset tight and settling her skirts over the cheap hoop. She was pinning on her bonnet, smoothing her wild curls as well as she could, when she heard the knock at the door.

"*Mabel!*" Ned roared.

Mabel sprinted downstairs. Before the second knock could come, she swung the door open.

"Hello," she said breathlessly. "It's so lovely to see you. What a nice surprise!"

She hoped that the words sounded sincere to the visitors on her doorstep. Ada Davies wore more powder and rouge than was proper, and her lips were painted an unconvincing pink. None of the above could hide her crooked teeth, bulging eyes, or the wrinkles etched above her plump cheeks.

"Mabel," she trilled. "How sweet of you. Don't you look nice today?"

She looked her up and down as she spoke and hesitated a moment too long over the word *nice*.

"Thank you," Mabel managed through tight lips. "Ned, darling, it's your sister and brother-in-law."

Ned shuffled through from the living room with a jovial pretence of surprise. Alf, Ada's long, thin husband, ignored Mabel completely. He pushed past her and went to shake Ned's hand.

"Good to see you, old fellow," he said. "I see you're still living in this old place."

Ned smiled, but his eyes were cold. "No rich fathers here, Alf."

"Nonsense, Neddy." Ada gave an annoying, whistling laugh. "Papa had a beautiful, big farm to leave to *you*." Her smile slipped on the last word.

"Tea?" Mabel asked.

"Of course they want tea," Ned snapped. "Bring it."

Mabel inclined her head and scrambled to the kitchen, where she retrieved the utensils used for their only visitors: a battered silver tray badly in need of polish that Ned would never buy for her, an ancient set of china cups and saucers, and some unconvincingly gilded spoons. As a child, Mabel had dreamed of having a real china tea set one day. Now, she hated these cups and saucers with a passion. They meant nothing but more work to her.

She arranged them on the tray, poured the tea, and fetched a box of real sugar cubes from the very back of the cupboard instead of using the honey they harvested on the farm. Still breathing hard, she carried the tray through to the sitting room.

Ada and Alf perched on their aging couch while Ned sagged in his usual armchair. His glowering eyes followed Mabel as she set the tray on the table.

"How about this drought, eh, old boy?" Alf asked jovially. "I know you farming chaps must be pulling out your hair."

"It's nothing this farm hasn't survived before," said Ned breezily.

"Sugar?" Mabel asked timidly.

"Three," said Alf.

"Where are all your pigs?" Ada asked. "I thought there were lots of them last time we were here."

Ned's smile curled up further, but his eyes narrowed. "Gone to market."

"It's that time of year for farming folks, dear," said Alf condescendingly.

"Of course." Ada patted his knee. "You're so clever, dear."

Mabel added a dash of freshly skimmed cream to Alf's tea, then handed it to him. He sneered at the teacup before taking it with a big, false smile. "Much obliged, Mabel."

"Sugar, Ada?" Mabel asked.

"Oh, just one or two," said Ada breezily. "No cream."

Mabel added two, stirred and handed her the teacup.

"What brings you to this part of the country?" Ned asked as Mabel handed him his own tea—sugar and cream.

"Why, I just wanted to see my little brother," said Ada. "I've missed you, dear. Are you coming to the Guy Fawkes party at our house? It's going to be simply *wonderful*."

Ned grunted. "Depends on the harvest."

Mabel sank timidly into a chair and sipped her own black, bitter tea.

"Of course. Depends on the harvest," said Alf sagely.

Footsteps clattered in the hallway. "Mr. Finch!" Anna cried in panic. "*Mr. Finch!*"

Ned flew to his feet, his face turning scarlet. Mabel was at the door before him; she put out her hands and tried to stop Anna from pushing into the room.

"Anna!" she hissed. "Not now."

"It's an emergency," Anna cried. She pushed past Mabel. "Mr. Finch, it's the horse. He's out of the paddock. He's running down the lane! I've sent a boy to stop him, but—"

"Get out of my way!" Ned barked.

He shoved Mabel aside, and Anna ran down the hall ahead of him as he stumped after her.

"I do apologize," Mabel squeaked to the Davies. "We'll be back in a moment."

"Why, it is rather chaotic here, isn't it?" Ada raised her eyebrows and delicately sipped tea.

Mabel cringed as she slowly shut the door. She hovered in the hallway, knowing that she should rush out and help to catch the loose horse. Yet she knew Ned would be in a fine temper. The shouting and cursing that lay ahead loomed like a mountain before her.

Her limbs felt weak. She hung her head, trying to find her courage.

"Ada, this isn't going to work," said Alf.

Mabel raised her head and frowned. What were they talking about?

"Nonsense," said Ada. "Of course it'll work."

"Look at this place," Alf snapped. "It's falling apart. Your brother is going to run it into the ground long before we can ever get our hands on it."

Mabel held her breath.

"We'll turn it around," said Ada.

"We don't have the money to turn it around," Alf hissed.

"Well, I'm not the one who squandered your fortune and got us hundreds of pounds in debt," said Ada.

Mabel tried not to gasp. In debt! But Alf and Ada always seemed so well-off.

"You certainly helped," Alf growled.

"Shhh," said Ada. "They'll be back any minute."

"Mabel!" Ned roared from outside.

Mabel hung her head. As always, she immediately responded to his summons.

*****

Sweat dripped into Mabel's eyes as she bent over the barley. She stretched her dry, chapped hands between the rows of grain for the umpteenth time that morning and wrapped her fingers around a thin and struggling weed, then wrenched it from the soil and placed it carefully on a piece of sacking beside her. They would feed it to the cow that evening; the poor beast's pasture was all but bare.

"Are you all right, Mabel?" Anna asked. "You look a little peaky."

"Fine," Mabel murmured.

She dragged a hand over her face, wiping away the stinging sweat, but more replaced it almost instantly. Mabel gritted her teeth and bent down to grip another weed.

"By Jove, it's hot," she murmured.

Anna shook her head. "It really isn't. You're the only one who's sweating. That's why I asked, dear."

Mabel looked up. Anna was right. Only her two children, both girls, still worked in the field with Mabel; Ned had laid off all the others. They moved in miserable silence, their agile young fingers pulling out weed after weed, but both wore coats.

"I just feel hot," said Mabel.

Anna's face pinched with worry. "Maybe you should sit down for a minute."

"No, no. I'm all right." Mabel straightened. "I just—"

She stopped as her head spun violently. Her vision swam, and she clapped a hand over her eyes, fighting against the nausea that lurched in her stomach.

"Mabel!" said Anna, but her voice seemed very distant.

Mabel tried to say something. Bile rose in her throat, and she gritted her teeth, fighting it down.

"Mabel!" Anna called again.

Her strong hands closed around Mabel's arm and gently tugged her away. Mabel was too weak to resist. She leaned on Anna, swallowing hard against her sick stomach, and allowed herself to be dragged to the stonewalled edge of the barley field.

"Sit, dear. Sit down," said Anna firmly.

Mabel's knees buckled. She sagged against the wall, and Anna unceremoniously thrust her head between her knees.

"There you are, pet." Anna rubbed her back. "Take deep breaths. It'll be over in a second."

Despite Mabel's misgivings, Anna was right. The spinning slowed and stopped. When she opened her eyes, her vision was clear again, although the sick feeling remained. Sweat cooled and dried on her skin.

"Here," said Anna. She held out a skin of water.

Mabel took it and rinsed out her mouth, then drank. Despite her thirst, she only managed two sips before her stomach gave a rebellious buck and its contents threatened to escape.

"It's all right," said Anna again.

"It's not all right," Mabel moaned. "Anna, I can't be sick now. I have to help with the harvest."

Anna tilted her head to one side. "Oh no, dear. I don't think you're sick at all. Quite the contrary."

Mabel raised her head, swallowing her nausea. "What do you mean?"

Anna crouched in the dry, crunching grass beside her and rested a hand on her shoulder. "Are you late, my pet?"

"Late?" Mabel asked.

Anna said nothing, but her stare was penetrating.

"Oh—*late*." Mabel raised a hand to her mouth, shock pulsing through her. "I... I don't know. It's been so busy with the harvest... I didn't..." She gulped. "Maybe."

Anna squeezed her shoulder. "You might be in the family way, my dear."

Family. Mabel pressed a hand over her belly, fear pulsing through her blood.

"How do I tell for sure?" she whispered.

"You'd have to ask the midwife, dear. I don't know," said Anna. "I never knew until my belly swelled." She smiled over at the children labouring in the field.

Horror clutched at Mabel's heart with a cold hand. She imagined her own child spending their entire life bent double in a field like this, and though she'd never seen her own life as appalling, the thought suddenly crushed her. What would Ned say? Would he be pleased? Would he be horrified? How would they feed a baby if the harvest failed?

Tears gathered at the corners of her eyes.

"Oh, pet." Anna rubbed her back. "Are you all right?"

Mabel lurched to her feet. The ground tilted briefly beneath her feet, but she denied her body its weakness and strode into the field.

"Mabel!" Anna called. "Where are you going?"

"The field needs weeding," Mabel mumbled. "We need to weed it now."

She bent and pulled the next weed from the furrow, trying to ignore the wild thundering of her heart.

Chapter Three

The house's yellow lanterns beckoned as Mabel stumbled from the barn to her home. She knew Ned would be furious that she hadn't been inside to make his tea, but the fear felt distant compared to the nausea rolling in her belly.

The nausea was worse in the mornings, but at night, after a full day in the fields, she felt shaky on her feet. She stumbled into the house, breathing heavily, and stopped to pour water from a jug and drink deeply. The water steadied her but made her stomach feel worse.

Mabel pressed her hands onto the kitchen table and hung her head, struggling to hold back the urge to curl up on the cold floor and sleep.

Was that twitch she felt a function of her hungry stomach, or a kick from a tiny life growing within?

She fought back the panic that threatened to enfold her, shoved down her exhaustion, and grasped the kettle. After hanging it over the fire, she checked on the stew she'd started earlier.

The meat and vegetables bubbled in a rich sauce that sent a waft of fragrance into the air. Mabel leaned closer—she loved the smell of beef stew. Now, though, the rich aroma made her stomach flip. She retreated hastily and replaced the lid.

Its clatter rang through the kitchen, but no answering yell came from deeper inside the home.

Mabel frowned. Usually, Ned would be screaming at her by now.

A ripple of worry spread through her. If something happened to Ned—

The thought was unbearable. It would be just as it had been when her parents died. She would be terrifyingly and totally alone.

The memory spurred her from the kitchen. "Ned?" she called. "Ned, dear, where are you?"

Ned didn't call out, but the scritch of a pen on paper caught her attention. Mabel whirled around and relief washed through her as she spotted him. He was in the sitting room, not in his usual armchair, but at the rickety and disused writing-desk by the window. The lantern on the desk provided a dull yellow glow over the page on the table.

"Ned?" Mabel entered the room softly, resisting the urge to touch her belly.

"I'm busy," Ned growled.

Mabel doubted she'd ever seen Ned write an entire page before. He did so laboriously, but the pen scratched out surprisingly neat letters in rows on the blank page, nearing the bottom.

"What are you doing?" Mabel asked softly.

Ned shook his head. "What do you think, woman? My barley's dying in the fields. My farm's on the rocks. Who knows what might happen next?"

His tone chilled her to the bones. *We might be having a baby next,* she thought, and shoved the idea away. "What are you writing?" she asked softly.

"Are you stupid, woman?" Ned barked.

Mabel looked away, fighting tears. "No," she said quietly, "but you know I can't read, dear."

She squeezed the pet name onto the end of the sentence, and it barely tempered Ned's annoyance. He snorted and turned back to the paper.

"I'm writing my will," he growled. "Leave me alone. I have to concentrate."

Mabel had already pushed her luck. She retreated quickly, tears stinging her eyes as she hurried to the kitchen. Why was Ned writing his will? She knew that was the document that told people what to do with someone's things when they died. She knew this because, in their will, her parents had left everything to her brother. And he had thrown her out of the house the second he could read it.

But he could read. Mabel couldn't.

She swallowed hard and stirred the stew once more, holding her breath against its savoury smell. She couldn't think of death or loss right now.

She might have to concentrate on something altogether different if Anna was right.

*****

Mabel sat very quietly on the wagon's front seat as the horse plodded along the lane toward town. The village was a wisp of smoke on the opposite hill. Mabel could hear church bells ringing; once again, they were too late to attend the service.

She forced away her anxiety over the matter and interlaced her fingers in her lap to keep herself from bringing her hands near her belly. When she glanced sideways at Ned, the man's face was puckered and scarlet. He scowled at the horse and snapped the whip in the air, making the animal go faster.

She scraped her courage together; his mood was no fouler than usual, and she'd delayed the question too long already. "Ned, dear." She cleared her throat. "Where, ah, where would you like to go when—"

"What's it to you, woman?" Ned snarled. "Get what you need for the house and I'll meet you at the wagon."

She fell silent, nodding apologetically, but he'd already given his answer. He was going to the inn.

That would buy her the time that she needed.

The wagon rattled over the cobblestones in the market square and Ned steered it to a quiet space near the market. He handed the reins to Mabel.

"Don't go feeding this horse, now," he barked. "You're spoiling the animal. There's not enough oats for the winter as it is."

"Yes, dear," said Mabel meekly, but the lie was bitter on her tongue.

Ned flung himself for the wagon and strode briskly for the inn. Even though she knew he wouldn't look around, Mabel waited until the door had swung shut behind him before she retrieved a nosebag of oats from beneath the seat and hung it over the horse's ears. She wondered if Ned had bothered to check the oats bin in the barn; if he had, he'd have known that there was more than enough for the winter. She'd made sure of it after the pigs were sold. They couldn't farm at all without the horse at full strength.

He nudged her as she patted his neck. "Wish me luck, old boy," she said. No one else seemed likely to do so.

Mabel paused at the edge of the market, watching as women moved between the stalls, selecting pumpkins and apples or sugar and flour. Should she shop first, or head for her real destination first? No, she had to go to the cottage on the corner before anything else. If Ned came out of the inn and found her shopping, he'd shout at her, but he wouldn't ask awkward questions.

Mabel inhaled deeply, turned toward the cottage on the square's corner, and strode toward it with all of her courage.

She glanced around the square as though walking over to old Mrs. Ackroyd's home was a suspicious activity of some kind. *Not at all*, she told herself. *No one will think twice about seeing you visit a dear old lady.* Still, her skin prickled when she reached the door and rapped briskly on it with her knuckles.

"Be a minute," a kindly voice called from within.

Mabel glanced at the inn. Its door was still firmly closed, and coarse laughter rose through the half-open windows.

Relief washed through her when the door opened to reveal Josephine Ackroyd, whose wrinkled old face lifted into a smile. "Oh, hello, Mrs. Finch. How are you?"

Mabel finally allowed herself to press a hand to her belly. "I don't know," she said tearfully.

Understanding dawned in Josephine's eyes. "Come in, dearie," she said. "We'll soon know."

She led Mabel to a cot in the kitchen, a place where many an ill or injured villager had been brought. Some said that Josephine was a witch, but she'd nursed Mabel's ailing parents, and Mabel knew her for what she truly was: an elderly widow who lived to help others. She had helped most of the village's babies into the world—and most of its elderly out of it.

Her examination was quick and gentle, with soft, cool hands. Mabel buttoned her dress tightly when it was over.

"When last have you been unwell, dearie?" Josephine asked gently.

Mabel shook her head. "I don't remember. It's been so busy."

"That's all right." Josephine laid a hand on her knee. "It's quite evident to me. You say you've been sick? Dizzy?"

Mabel nodded.

"Then I think you may be quite certain that you're in a delicate condition." Josephine beamed. "You've been married a year, have you? This is lovely, dear. You must tell your husband quickly. He'll be so delighted."

Mabel swallowed. She wasn't sure about that.

She barely heard Josephine's words about giving in to her cravings and making arrangements for her confinement as she slipped to her feet and stumbled to the door. The old woman grasped her arm and squeezed it lightly, her eyes dancing amid their bed of wrinkles.

"Congratulations, dearie," she said. "Your life is about to become very rich and wonderful."

"Thank you," Mabel managed.

Josephine inclined her head, gave her arm another squeeze, and shut the door.

Mabel stood on the pavement outside the cottage, shivering in the cold breeze that whisked between the cottages and howled briskly across the square, rattling tablecloths on the stalls. It felt as though that breeze blew through the centre of her being, sending ribbons of cold into her fingers and toes. She stared down at her corseted belly. It seemed so ordinary, but hadn't she realized that she could no longer pull her corset so tight? Hadn't she noticed the tension of cloth over her midriff?

Terror clumped in her throat. *I'm having a baby. Oh, my poor, poor baby. What am I going to do?*

The tears spilled from her throat to her eyes, then down her cheeks in a hot stream.

She struggled against them, but couldn't make them stop. Mabel raised a hand to her face in a bid to hide her terror from those around her.

"Mrs. Finch, isn't it?"

The shocking gentleness of the voice almost dried her tears. Mabel wiped her eyes hurriedly, then looked up into the gentle face of Percy Mitchell.

"That's right." Mabel sniffed.

Percy kept his distance, hands in his pockets, but a wrinkle appeared between his eyebrows. "Are you quite well, Mrs. Finch? Do you need assistance?"

Yes, Mabel screamed inwardly. *Please. Help me.* But it was almost not proper for her to speak to Percy, let alone admit her terror to him.

She hastily dried her eyes on her sleeve and forced a smile. She wondered when last she had truly smiled; it seemed that the only purpose for the expression was to don a disarming mask, to make herself harmless.

"I'm quite all right," she whispered. "Thank you very much."

"All right," said Percy reluctantly. His eyes held hers. "If you're quite sure."

"I am," Mabel lied. "Thank you."

He doffed his hat to her and strolled away, and Mabel's heart pounded as she watched him go. Even as her heart cried out for his help, she knew that it would not be forthcoming from any quarter.

She would have to do this alone.

*****

"Are you all right, dearie?" the baker's wife asked. She tilted her head to one side in concern as Mabel pushed a few coins across the counter to her.

Mabel was sick of hearing those words. More than that, she was just sick; her stomach boiled even in the presence of the bakery's delicious smells.

"Fine, thank you," she mumbled.

She took the brown paper bag of the sticky sweet buns that Ned liked so much, praying that she'd made the right choice by buying them. They seldom failed at tempering Ned's anger and giving Mabel a blessed evening of peace. But then again, they cost more than a whole bag of flour that she could use to make many loaves of bread at home.

Maybe he would be angry about the money, or maybe, she thought, he would be too drunk to care.

"*Mabel*!"

Mabel jumped. It seemed that the latter was possible as Ned stormed from the inn, swaying hideously as he made his way towards her. His scarlet face and bulging eyes made her heart skip. He seemed wobblier on his feet than usual.

"N-Ned?" Mabel stammered.

"What are you standing there for?" Ned roared. "Have you finished the shopping?"

Mabel scraped together her courage. She would simply have to make the best of it.

"Yes," she said. "I've finished. Look—I bought these lovely buns you like." She held up the paper bag, allowing the scent to escape despite the heave of her gut.

"I don't care. Get in the wagon!" Ned shouted. "We're going home."

Mabel hugged the bag to her chest and scampered to the wagon. The horse dozed between the shafts, still harnessed. She'd taken off his nosebag earlier to hide it from Ned. His eyes snapped wide when Ned scrambled onto the driver's seat, knowing what was coming next. Before her husband could seize the whip, the horse jumped forward, jerking the wagon so that Mabel almost fell as she tried to scramble up.

"Come on, woman," Ned barked impatiently.

"I'm sorry, dear," said Mabel.

She huddled on the driver's seat as Ned hauled on the reins. The horse swung around, then kept turning as Ned pulled and pulled, dragging the wagon in a circle.

"Ned, look out!" Mabel cried.

The back of the wagon collided with a stall selling fruit. The woman behind the table scrambled out of the way, but the table tipped, spilling bouncing fruit in all directions.

"Hey!" she cried.

"Sorry!" Mabel called. "I'm sorry. Ned, dear—"

"Get up!" Ned barked, slapping the horse's haunches sharply with the whip.

The animal lunged against his collar, snorting, jaws agape as he tried to fathom the confusing jerks of Ned's hands.

He ignored a hard yank to the left, bless him, and plunged toward the lane out of the village in panic.

"Easy, Ned!" Mabel cried.

Ned brandished the whip at her. "Silence, woman!"

Mabel clutched the seat as the horse set off at a half-trot, half-canter, snorting and gasping with terror. Two wheels bounced off the road and made the wagon lurch. Mabel almost pitched off her seat, and a terrifying thought gripped her: *What if I'd been holding a baby?*

She swallowed hard and glanced at Ned. His jaws were slack with drink, and he whipped the horse again, driving him faster despite the bend at the end of the lane.

"Ned," she whimpered.

Ned whirled to face her. Saliva sprayed her face as he screamed, "When will you be *silent*, woman?"

"Ned, the turn!" Mabel cried.

Ned's eyes widened as the stone wall following the lane rushed toward them. He seized the reins and yanked hard on one, ripping the horse's head to one side. The panicking, blinkered animal could see nothing. He tried to slow, but the speeding wagon rammed hard against the breeching on his hindquarters, and sheer weight and speed bore him onward.

Mabel didn't scream. All she could think of was the tiny life within her, innocent of the world's terrors. She threw the brown paper bag aside as the horse galloped sideways and pell-mell toward the wall. Time slowed, and her certainly became absolute. She gathered herself and sprang from the wagon as two of its wheels left the ground. For a second, she floated in the air, curiously free.

Then she was falling and the splinter of woods and screaming of the horse filled her ears. She threw her arms around her body and curled up tightly, then hit the ground hard on her shoulder. She skidded for an instant. There was just enough time to feel relief that she hadn't landed on her belly when her head smacked against the road and everything went dark.

*****

When Mabel opened her eyes, it was to the horse's screams. Wood cracked and desperate hooves scrabbled on stone. Her vision spun for a second, but as she scrambled to her hands and knees, it cleared and she could see the scene of the accident.

The wagon lay upside down, its cast-iron undercarriage brutally exposed, wheels still turning. Amid shattered wood and broken leather, the horse lay on his back in the ditch, hooves kicking helplessly against the stone wall.

Ned was underneath the wagon. Only his head and chest protruded; the heavy wood lay over his belly and legs. Blood smeared his forehead. His hat was gone, and his rich blond hair sprayed over the ruined grass.

"Ned!" Mabel screamed.

She stumbled to her feet. Her shoulder throbbed, but her belly was fine. She kept a protective arm wrapped around it as she ran to her fallen husband's side.

"Ned, Ned, Ned," she gasped. She fell to her knees beside him and cupped her hands around his cheeks.

His breaths came in damp rattles. Blood sprayed on her wrists, and his eyes were glassy, staring.

"Ned, please," Mabel cried.

The breaths stopped coming.

"*Ned*!" Mabel screamed.

"Mabel!"

The pure, soft voice rang out and dragged her attention from the body of the man she'd been married to. Percy sprinted down the lane toward her, a crowd of concerned villagers close on his heels. He was the first to reach them by several yards, and he grabbed Mabel's shoulders.

"Look out!" he cried.

Wood splintered. The panicking horse had almost freed himself, and his iron-rimmed hooves flew only feet away from Mabel.

The world was spinning as Percy dragged her away from the fallen wagon, his hands warm, strong, and tender on her shoulders. She tried to squirm away from him nonetheless as a crush of villagers crowded around Ned.

"Ned," she croaked.

Percy put an arm around her shoulders and held her up. "Are you hurt?"

Mabel touched the bloodied spot on her shoulder, then shook her head dumbly.

"Doctor!" Percy cried. "She's hurt!"

The village doctor had long whiskers and a jowly face. He barely glanced at Mabel, then ran through the crowd to get to Ned.

"He'll tend to you in a minute," said Percy. "Just a minute."

"It happened so fast." Mabel's breaths rasped, and her knees gave way. "It all happened so fast."

Percy lowered her to the grassy verge, and she sat on a knoll, staring.

Josephine wheezed up to her, leaning on a cane. "Mabel, dear, are you—"

"I'm not hurt," said Mabel.

Josephine clutched her shoulder.

The doctor straightened slowly. Through the crush of legs, Mabel saw only a tangled mop of Ned's hair.

When the doctor turned toward Mabel, she read the answer to her question in his limp hands and sagging shoulders even before he came to her and said the words. Her ears were ringing so loudly that she didn't hear them, but she knew what he said. She knew that Ned was gone.

He would never scream at her again. He was gone, just like her parents, and he'd taken the whole world with him.

"Mabel?"

The soft touch on her arm awakened her. Mabel raised her head as Percy leaned over her.

"Did you hear the doctor?" he asked.

"Yes," said Mabel. "Ned is dead."

"I'm afraid so, Mabel, but what he said was that your shoulder is only grazed," said Percy. "Your arm will be all right."

Mabel blinked at her shoulder. When had she taken off her coat?

"Perhaps you should come home with me, pet," said Josephine. "I don't think you should be alone."

The world washed over Mabel. Wave after wave, it threatened to pull her under and drown her.

But no. It couldn't. Her arm tightened around her belly, and something flared inside her—something that had never been there before.

Mabel shook her head slowly. "No, thank you, Josephine." She spoke clearly, her voice calm and steady, her eyes dry.

"Are you sure?" Josephine asked.

Mabel cleared her throat. She spotted her coat lying nearby and donned it against the autumn chill, feeling the faint tug of pain in her shoulder. Then she straightened in a smooth movement. There was no sign of the horse, but the ruined wagon still lay in the road. Someone had put a sheet over the body.

The body. That was all it was now.

"Doctor," said Mabel, "would you kindly speak to the undertaker?" She reached for her purse and took out a few of their last coins. "I would be pleased if he would take the body away and make the funeral arrangements."

The doctor nodded. "Very well."

"What else do you need help with?" Percy asked gently.

"Where is the horse?" Mabel asked.

"Lame, I'm afraid. They've led him to Farmer Hoggart's barn across the road," said Percy.

"Very well. I shall speak to Farmer Hoggart," said Mabel. "Perhaps he can help me to repair the wagon, too." She smoothed her skirt.

"Mrs. Finch, you're in shock," said the doctor.

"I am quite all right, doctor." Mabel squared her shoulders. "Mr. Mitchell?"

"Yes?" said Percy.

"My husband left a will," said Mabel. "I shall collect it and bring it to town as soon as I can. Would you be able to read it for me?"

"Of course. Anything you need," said Percy.

Mabel allowed herself to touch his arm briefly with her shaking fingers. "Thank you," she managed. "Th-thank you."

"I'll take you home in my carriage," said Percy.

"That—that won't be necessary." Mabel squared her shoulders. "The walk will do me good. Thank you very much."

She spotted the brown paper bag of buns lying nearby, miraculously intact, and lifted it. It would do for dinner. Then she clamped it under her arm, raised her chin, and strode toward home.

Chapter Four

Mabel ate lunch the next day quietly on her own and in the kitchen.

It was the first time she felt she could eat that day. The bubbling nausea gave her few opportunities, and she picked slowly at a single bun, staring out of the window. It was such a nice day. The birds that swooped and darted amid the branches seemed so cheerful.

Yet the paddock was so empty. They had shot the horse. His leg was broken.

Mabel wondered if she was a monster for feeling more sorrow about the horse than about Ned. The ringing silence in the house was so strange, and yet no one had called her names or pushed her that day, and it was a strange feeling.

She sat in the kitchen with lunch, chewing slowly, not knowing how to feel. Frightened, of course. After lunch she would take Ned's will to Percy and then she would find out if she was pregnant and destitute. Or just completely alone with a farm, a failing crop, and a baby on the way.

Mabel touched her belly. Percy would help, she knew. With his help, maybe she and her baby would be all right.

She finished the bun, washed her hands, and went into the living room. Earlier that day, she'd taken the will from Ned's desk drawer—at least, she hoped it was his will. She couldn't read the title at the top, only vaguely make out the shape of her late husband's name, Edgar Joseph Finch.

Percy would help, she told herself. Percy would help.

She turned to get her coat and the knock at the door was so startling that the will's papers spilled from her hands. Gasping, Mabel fell to her knees and scrambled to gather them.

The knock came again. Maybe it was Anna, Josephine, or even Percy, come to help her.

"I'll be there in a minute!" Mabel called.

She finally gathered the papers and set them on the writing desk, then hastened to the front door. She prepared a smile before pulling it wide.

"Oh, Mabel!" Ada Davies cried. "Oh, Mabel, Mabel, Mabel, my poor, poor little brother!"

Mabel gasped, but had no time to avoid the woman. Ada flung herself on Mabel's shoulder, wailing, and clung to her tightly. Powder smeared on Mabel's cheek and she reeled under her sister-in-law's weight.

"Neddy's gone!" Ada screamed in Mabel's ear. "How can he be gone?" She fell against Mabel and poured theatric tears over the front of her dress.

"A-Ada?" Mabel croaked. "What are you doing here?" She patted the woman's shoulder in a bid to make her let go.

"What do you think we're doing here?" Alf demanded, shouldering his way into the house. "Her brother has just passed away, and come to find out, his widow didn't have the decency to let her know!"

Mabel's cheeks burned. "I'm so sorry," she said quietly. "It was all such a shock."

"Oh, Alfie, *darling*." Ada straightened, still clutching Mabel around the shoulders. "Don't be so rude to poor Mabel. Can you imagine how awful it must have been? Were you on the wagon with him, Mabel, dear?"

Mabel struggled with an unexpected wave of tears. "I was."

"It's a miracle you weren't hurt," said Ada. "It's an utter miracle. Oh, Alfie, darling, how awful it must be for her! How absolutely awful! And our town is *miles* away."

Alf snorted. "You could have written."

Mabel's cheeks warmed still more. "I couldn't have," she said quietly.

"Whyever not?" Alf demanded.

"Yes, why not, Mabel?" Ada's tears welled up all the faster. "I'm sure Neddy provided you with everything you need. Oh, my poor Neddy! Such a husband! He would have been such a good father!"

The words stung deep in Mabel's soul.

"I'm sorry," she said quietly. "I couldn't write to you because I can't read."

Alf looked unsurprised, but Ada bridled suddenly. "You can't *read*? My Neddy married a girl who can't *read*?"

Mabel stared at the woman, at the powder smeared across her cheek. "No. I can't."

"My oh my!" Ada cried.

"Now, now, Ada." Alf's shrewd gaze swept the room. "I know all this is a horrid shock for everybody. Why don't we all sit down and have a cup of tea while we work it all out? There'll be a funeral to attend. Mabel may need help with the funeral arrangements."

Mabel blinked in surprise. It startled her that Alf knew her name, let alone would extend this small gesture of kindness to her.

"I'll make the tea," she said.

She left Alf and Ada in the sitting room and hurried to the kitchen, where she hung the kettle over the fire. Something about having them in the sitting room on their own made her skin crawl. She had to resist the urge to check on them as though worried they'd steal her cheap silverware.

As Mabel poured the tea, she scolded herself for being silly and fanciful. Why would Alf and Ada do such a thing? They had plenty of money...

Or did they? She thought back to the argument she'd overheard. *Hundreds of pounds in debt.*

She grabbed the tea tray with shaking hands, not caring when she spilled a little cream, and hastened to the sitting room. Alf sat on the high-backed armchair—Ned's armchair— while Ada perched on the couch, crying hard into her handkerchief. The silver was where it always was, in the cabinet by the writing desk, and Mabel chided herself again for being suspicious.

"Ada, it's all right," she said gently. "Come on, now. Dry your eyes. Here's some tea; it'll make you feel better."

Ada raised her head, powder and paint running down her cheeks from weeping. "I can't bear it, Mabel. I can't bear Ned being gone."

"I'm sorry," said Mabel. She didn't know what else to say.

She set the tray down and turned to Alf.

"Mabel, look what I found," he said. He held up the pages she'd just collected from the floor. "It's Ned's will."

"I saw him writing it just a few days ago," said Mabel. She swallowed an unexpected lump in her throat. "I'm taking it to Mr. Mitchell, the lawyer in town, to read to me. I'm sure he'll know what to do with it."

"Well, there's no need for that." Alf shook out the page.

Ada was suddenly very quiet. She clutched her teacup in both hands, staring intently at her husband.

"I'm perfectly capable of reading the will for you, aren't I?" said Alf.

Mabel hesitated. She had almost been looking forward to going to town to see Percy... Then she pushed the thought aside, shame boiling in her belly. *What's wrong with you, Mabel? Ned's body is hardly cold.*

She cleared her throat. "Thank you very much, Alf. That would be wonderful."

"Very well. Let's see what he says here." Alf cleared his throat and peered at the page through his monocle. "This is the last will and testament of Edgar Joseph Finch, birth date, and so on and so forth... ah... I see... Yes."

Mabel's stomach tied itself in knots. She stood by the tea table, sipping from her cup as gently as she could, but she slopped some of the liquid over the rim. Surely the farm would be hers. Surely Ned would have left it to her. He had no brothers, no other male relatives. Surely, surely, she would be able to make a living here in the place that had become her home.

"Aha. Yes. All right, then." Alf read to the end of the page, then lowered it to his lap. "Well, Mabel, Ned's will—may he rest in peace—is really quite simple."

Mabel glanced in confusion at the two pages. Didn't that take a lot of words? Then again, what did she know?

"Wh-what does it say?" she tremored.

Ada was very silent. She stared at Mabel with intense eyes.

"The will has only one beneficiary," said Alf.

"What does that mean?" Mabel asked.

Alf stared down his nose at her. "It means that Ned left everything to only one person."

Mabel swallowed. "He–he did?"

"Yes," said Alf.

"Who?" Mabel croaked. *Me. It has to be me. Please, let it be me,* she prayed. *Let me raise my baby here in peace.*

"Me," said Alf.

Mabel's mind stuttered to a halt. "I—I beg your pardon?"

"It's quite simple, Mabel. Of course Ned wanted his farm to go to his dear older sister Ada." Alf gestured at her as though Mabel might not know who she was. "Since Ada is married to me, I am the legal owner of her property. Therefore, Ned's farm belongs to me. Well, to Ada and I." Alf smiled. "It's very, very simple."

Mabel's knees gave way under her. She sagged onto her chair, and suddenly she went back in time three years to the morning she found her parents dead in their room in an empty, echoing house. The home around her was no longer her home, she knew.

Ned had left her and taken everything with him. Leaving the farm to Ada was his last act of cruelty toward her. His last abuse.

Ada laughed, a horrible, braying sound. "Did you think he'd left the farm to *you*?"

"Maybe," Mabel croaked.

Ada laughed again. "Oh, Mabel, you must be in terrible shock if you'd think so. Ned would never do such a thing." Her eyes filled with tears again. "He loved *me*. He loved me more than anything."

"Yes, quite right, my dear," said Alf.

Mabel wrapped her arms around her body, hugging her belly, her unborn baby whose future now hung so tenuously in the balance.

"Oh, don't look so horrified, Mabel." Ada crossed the room and sat on the couch beside Mabel. When she put an arm around her shoulders, she squeezed so hard that the bruise on Mabel's shoulder stung.

"I've lost everything," Mabel whispered. "My home… everything."

Alf and Ada exchanged a pointed glance.

"Of course you haven't lost your home, darling," said Ada.

Mabel raised her head. "I haven't?"

"No." Ada smiled. "Why would we chase you off the farm? You belong here. You're still family, after all."

Mabel stared at the woman's painted face and guilt grew even larger in her stomach. Why had she presumed that Alf and Ada would cruelly insist on throwing her off the farm? They were good people. They *were* family, after all.

She ignored the niggling through that her brother—who had inherited everything her parents owned—had done exactly that.

"I'll work," she said quickly. "I'll work to earn my keep. I know the farm well. I can help you. I know farming. I promise I'll work."

"Oh, yes," said Alf quietly. "You certainly shall."

*****

The nausea and dizziness clutching at Mabel, as it did every morning, was pitiful now compared to the pain and grief that assailed her. She belt over the barley as they weeded the last field, trying not to cry. The thick lump in her throat made no sense; her emotions seemed to be as wild and unruly as a stormy sea. One moment she thought, guiltily, that perhaps she was better off without Ned. The next she could barely breathe from agony.

What's wrong with you, Mabel? she wondered as she crouched to pluck more weeds from the dry ground.

"Are you sure you're all right, pet?" Anna asked her for the umpteenth time that morning. "Perhaps you should go inside and sit down."

"I'm fine," said Mabel faintly.

"You're white as a sheet," said Anna. "Please. We'll finish this field by lunchtime, you know that. It's best for you to rest when you need it."

Mabel raised her head. "I can't rest, Anna."

The older woman paused, compassion in her eyes. "Why not?"

"Because then Alf and Ada will start to ask questions," said Mabel.

Anna's expression darkened. "Them two townies."

It was only five days after Ned's death, but apparently that was enough time for Alf and Ada to bring their possessions from their larger house in town and cram it all into the poor little farmhouse, which was now unrecognizable.

"What a pair of fools!" said Anna. "Ned would have done much better to leave the farm to you, pet."

"Well, he didn't," said Mabel.

Anna watched her for a few moments as they worked together. "They don't know yet, do they?" she asked quietly. "About the baby."

Technically, Anna didn't know yet, either. Mabel hadn't breathed a word of her visit to Josephine. But these things had a way of circulating in the village, and Ned's gruesome, public death had left the Finches the talk of the town, to Mabel's dismay.

Mabel swallowed. "No," she whispered. "They don't."

"Poor lamb." Anna shook her head. "They're going to find out, you know."

"I know," said Mabel. *But maybe not now. Maybe not today.* Maybe today she could have one more normal day, and maybe tomorrow, too.

She was faint and dizzy when lunchtime came. Despite her slow work, as Anna had said, the field was done. Mabel trudged back to the farmhouse on legs that felt like her bones had turned to water.

It was a long walk. Her parched throat urged her to the water pitcher as soon as she reached the kitchen. She was still gulping hungrily from the cup, ignoring the queasy bouts of protest from her belly, when the shout rang from the sitting room.

"*Mabel!*"

She lowered the cup. Except for the feminine inflection, the voice could have been Ned's, screaming at her to get lunch ready. She felt a pang of both fury and sorrow and didn't know how to feel them at the same time.

"Mabel!" Ada screamed again.

Mabel composed herself with a deep breath and went through to the sitting room.

"I'm sorry, Ada," she began. "I've not started on lunch yet because—"

"Never mind the lunch," Ada barked. "Sit down."

Mabel blinked. Ada had never used that tone with her before. Alf sat in Ned's armchair, as usual, and Ada was on the couch. Her gaze pinned Mabel to the wall.

Alf regarded Mabel with a deep frown. The faux friendliness had left his face completely. Mabel had never realized how cold his eyes could be.

"Do as she says, Mabel," he said sharply.

Mabel shuffled to the nearest stool and sank onto it. The relief of having her weight off her feet was quickly crushed by terror.

"Why didn't you tell us about the barley?" Alf demanded.

"What about the barley?" Mabel asked.

"The fact that there's almost none!" Ada yelled.

"Ada, please." Alf extended a hand. "What my wife means to say is that our banker came by to value the barley crop."

His eyes narrowed. "He called it half of the usual yield for this farm."

"That's right," said Mabel. "If you recall, I've been telling you about the drought for some time now, and—"

"Drought? Why should the drought matter? You sowed the same amount of seeds, didn't you?" Ada demanded.

Mabel blinked. "Well, yes, but if the plant doesn't get enough rain, it doesn't matter that—"

Alf raised a hand. "You mean to tell me that my banker his correct." His voice began to tremble. "The barley crop will be half its usual yield."

"If we're lucky," said Mabel. "The drought has been terrible."

Ada cried out and clutched her chest. Alf studied Mabel over steepled fingers.

"I see," he murmured. "Well, this does complicate matters." He sighed. "I'm afraid I must ask you to leave, Mabel."

Shock shot through Mabel's belly like lightning. "L-leave?"

"That's right. I would like you to remove yourself from my premises." Alf raised his chin. "Before nightfall."

Dizziness gripped Mabel. She seized the edge of the stool to keep from falling.

"But why?" she moaned.

"Well, it's quite simple," said Alf. "If the barley harvest is so poor, the farm will make almost no money this year. Ada and myself, you see, are accustomed to a certain standard of living."

"You won't take it from us," Ada hissed.

"Nobody can take it from us, dear. Mabel is a guest in this house," said Alf. "I should say, *was* a guest in our house. You understand, Mabel, this is my home now."

Mabel gulped against nausea. "Please, Alf, you know how hard I work. I don't ask for wages. I'll sleep in the barn, too." She thought of the tiny life growing within her and the long winter ahead. "I'll live on scraps. I'll—"

"We want you gone!" Ada flew to her feet. "Don't you understand? We want you to leave and this is our home, so you have to leave. You don't have a choice!"

The words were terribly, appallingly true. Mabel rose, struggling to hold back her sobs. "I beg you," she said. "Please, I beg of you, I have nowhere else to go. I'll work more than ever. I'll do all your cooking, all your cleaning. I'll—"

"It is time for you to leave, Mabel," said Alf coolly. "Fetch your things from your room. I would prefer not to see you again."

Mabel stepped toward Alf. "Alf, please—"

Ada lunged. Her hands closed around Mabel's shoulders, nails digging into her skin. Mabel cried out as the woman pinned her against the wall. "*You have to leave!*" she shrieked. Her eyes were unstable orbs rolling in her powdered face.

Mabel's heart thudded against her chest. She thought of her baby, her poor little fatherless baby, and the violence in Ada's eyes was terrifying.

"All right!" she cried. "I'm leaving. I'm leaving!"

Ada released her. "*Go!*" she screamed.

Mabel almost fell. She struggled to her feet instead, breaths gasping. Her eyes darted to her room, but when Ada took a belligerent step closer, she knew that there was no chance to stop and take the few things she owned—some soap, a change of clothes, and a warm blanket.

She would have to do without those things. She would have to do without everything, she realized.

"Go!" Ada barked.

Confusion and terror drove Mabel to a run. She turned and bolted from the farmhouse door, then fled toward the village, tears rolling hot down her cheeks.

*****

Mabel only slowed when she reached the village.

Hunger clawed her belly as she limped into the abandoned market square. A few chickens pecked around the cobbles; a housewife swept her doorstep, humming to herself. Her tangible happiness made Mabel feel sick.

Help, she realized. She needed help. But from whom? Her gaze wandered to Josephine's door, but she knew that the old widow was penniless herself. No, Josephine wouldn't be able to help her.

Percy's face filled Mabel's thoughts. A scarlet flush crept over her cheeks, and she turned her head away as though that would make her escape them. She pressed her hands into her pockets, and something jingled lightly at her touch.

Mabel fumbled in her pocket and drew two small coins to the light. A few pennies. They were still in her pocket from when she'd been shopping only a few days ago, when Ned died. It felt like a lifetime had passed since then.

A distant shriek caught her attention. Mabel looked up from the pennies and saw a plume of white steam streaking across the autumn landscape. The cold gleam of the train was harsh and unnatural against the golden fields and barren trees, but she knew instantly what it meant.

The train went to London, a place with thousands upon thousands of people, a place of factories, docks, and shipyards where hundreds of ordinary folk like her worked every day. She personally knew of several people who'd moved to London for work. "They'll even let girls work in the factories," one man had told Ned at the market a few weeks ago.

Mabel's hand closed over the pennies. The man had said the words with disgust, but to her, they shone with golden opportunity. If she could find work in a factory, she could perhaps feed herself and her little one.

Determination flared in her at the thought of the child. She tilted her head back, squared her shoulders, and exhaled. It was time to leave this town and its gossipers behind. She looked neither left nor right, stopped for nothing, and said no goodbyes. She simply walked straight to the train station and bought their cheapest ticket to London.

*****

The journey was longer than Mabel had expected. Crowded into an airless box car with dozens of others, all standing, she'd been unable to feel safe. It was a mercy, perhaps, that there was nothing in her pockets. More than once, she felt a hand brush against her apron.

Terror drove her to a corner, where she wrapped her arms around herself and tried to ignore the hubbub of conversation and the steady huffing of the train. Every time the whistle shrieked, it made her jump.

Darkness sank over the world by the time the train screeched and puffed to a halt and the conductor finally called, "London." A crowd of people shuffled from the box car, bringing Mabel with them.

She allowed the tide to bear her out of the bustling train station and stumbled to a halt on the pavement of a market square, but this one was very different to the pleasant little square in the village back home.

Here, there were no chickens and no merry housewives. Instead, stalls crowded close on the cobblestones, of which there were several missing. Smoke rose from closely tended pots as thin old women displayed scoops of watery broth or grey gruel, shouting their pitiful prices for a bowlful. An ancient, bony donkey, the likes of which Mabel had never seen in the country, stumbled across the square dragging a sad cart cobbled together with bits old wood and string. The man driving the cart was as thin as the donkey, and it was filled with rags and bits of bone.

A terrible chill ran through Mabel. This was meant to be the land of opportunity, a place where she could raise her child safely. But when she raised her head to look up at the sky, she saw no stars at all. Only the choking darkness of smoke belching from a hundred factory chimneys.

"Flowers, missus?" someone whispered. "Nice fresh flowers from the hothouse."

Mabel looked down. The tiny girl standing at her feet was no bigger than six or seven. She clutched a fistful of sad, wilting blossoms. Their colour was as faded as if London had leached the beauty from them.

"Ha'penny a bunch," the girl croaked. She gave a terrible, wet cough into her elbow and blood splattered her dress.

Mabel reeled away. "What have I done?" she cried. "Oh, what have I done?"

She clasped her hands over her belly, heart pounding as she thought of the tiny life inside her. The flower girl kept coughing in nasty hacks and Mabel turned and fled. She jogged across the square, praying that this was simply the bad part of London, that she would find somewhere nice around the next corner.

When she reached the next street, she saw only dozens of factories crowded close around the narrow strip of cobbles. The air was thick with smoke here; it reeked more than anything Mabel had ever smelled before. It felt like she was breathing noxious fumes instead of normal air. Though it was late and dark, an hour at which country folk would be gathered around the fire, the factories thumped and clattered on. Mabel peered through the window of the nearest one to see if it was true, if they really did let women work in factories, and despite the stench, hope kicked in her chest.

This factory was filled with women and girls. They crowded around great, steaming vats, bent over tables covered in boxes, and hurried to and fro carrying wooden crates. There were hundreds of them in this building alone, all hard at work.

Perhaps she could work here. She glanced at the sign over the door. This place made matches; that seemed nice enough. She leaned closer to the glass, peering at the four girls assembled around a large vat near her, wherein some thick, tarry liquid bubbled. The girls were using racks to dip rows of matchsticks in the mixture. It had to be sulphur, Mabel guessed.

It looked like hot, hard, exhausting work, but Mabel was used to that. Hadn't she experienced it every day in the fields?

Then the girl nearest her raised her head, and shock made Mabel reel backwards.

The girl's face was hopelessly disfigured. A heavy black mass clung to her bottom jaw, distorting her eyes and dragging wrinkles in her cheeks. Something oozed from the mass, bringing white flecks with it.

Bone, Mabel realized. *Those are chips of bone.*

Horror clawed her belly. She staggered away from the alley, appalled and nauseated. If she had eaten anything since breakfast, she would have vomited. As it was, she merely doubled over and heaved, the dry retches cramping her belly muscles.

Her trembling legs carried her to the nearest alley, where she collapsed with her back to the grimy wall of the horrifying factory, her knees drawn up to her chest. She hugged herself tightly, sobbing the same words over and over to the poor baby she'd brought to this place.

"I'm so sorry. I'm so, so sorry."

Part Two

Chapter Five

Six Months Later

Mabel couldn't help shuddering as she shook the filthy sack over the table in front of her. Old hessian dust stung her nostrils, but it was nothing compared to the smell rising from the sack's contents.

As she shook, clumps of mouldy rags fell onto the table. They were disgusting scraps scavenged from the streets by the rag-and-bone men who worked for the factory. Some came from slop-shops or millineries who sold them as waste products.

Others were simply dug out of the rubbish. Mabel suspected that this was one such bag.

At least the nausea had faded over the six months she'd been in London. She doubted her stomach would have been able to handle the smell rising from the table as she tossed the sack aside for the men to collect later.

Now, she gazed down at the pile of rags, and felt only a twinge of disgust at the dusty, sticky mess. Bugs crawled over their surface, darting away when she extended her hands toward the pile.

She braced herself and plunged her hands into the mess. The quickest way to do this was to grab the smallest rags first and sort them into piles. The cleaner ones—which were stained, but not covered in excrement or lice—she tossed into a bin across the table. From there, men would take them away to be pulped into paper.

The truly disgusting rags went into the much larger bin behind her, and they would be thoroughly steamed before they ended up suffering the same fate.

A large group of women surrounded the table. None of them spoke; their eyes were on their work, quiet and obedient, hands moving quickly. Mabel ducked her head and tried her best to keep up even though the curve of her belly was in her way now. She had to pause periodically to brush mould, filth, and lice from her dress.

I'm sorry, baby, she thought, as she did a thousand times each day.

She shifted her weight, trying to ease the pressure on her aching, swollen ankles. Moving was much more difficult these days. She knew that her feet would be thickly swollen by the time her shift was over late that night.

One of the women across from her looked up, and her eyes flickered. Mabel's body tensed. She lowered her head and worked fast, her hands flying over the filthy cloths.

She heard the footsteps a moment later. In the gloomy, airless room, lit by a row of gas lamps, they echoed. Their supervisor was approaching.

"What's this?" he barked.

All the women flinched as though he'd laid a lash over their shoulders.

"What are you all doing?" the man demanded. "Do you think you get paid so generously to hang around here chattering?"

None of the women said a word. Tears of terror stung Mabel's eyes as she tossed clean rags into the bin opposite the table.

The supervisor's cane tapped on the ground as he strolled around the table. She dared not look up at him. He was a tall, gaunt figure with sallow skin and yellowed eyes, and he always carried that dreaded cane, a fashionable one, knobbly and uneven. Hard on the knuckles.

"What's this?" the man barked, leaning over the bin of clean rags.

The women worked even faster; a young girl beside Mabel was almost sobbing. The man lifted a rag from the bin with the end of his cane. He held it up for all to see the single louse crawling over the fabric.

Mabel's breath caught. *No... no. Please*.

"Who did this?" the supervisor yelled.

The women cowered.

The supervisor turned and flung the rag. Mabel threw up her hands with a yelp, narrowly keeping it from hitting her face.

"It was you," the man hissed, "wasn't it, you lazy wretch?" He jabbed her belly with the cane. "You think this will get you leniency?"

"No, sir. Of course not, Mr. Compton, sir," Mabel yelped.

"Silence!" Mr. Compton bellowed.

The women cringed.

"Empty this bin, you fat cow," Mr. Compton hissed. "Sort it all again."

Dismay flooded Mabel.

"But sir, it's already past eight in the evening," the new girl said. "She'll end up staying till midnight, and—"

Mr. Compton spun around and slammed his cane down. The girl screamed and yanked her hands away, her knuckles red.

"I asked for silence," he hissed. "This is a place for work. Now *work*!"

Mabel hurried around the table to shovel armfuls of rags from the bin. Mr. Compton stepped back, arms folded, and watched. A smug smile stretched across his bony face as she bent over the bin repeatedly, trying to pretend that her belly wasn't in the way, trying to pretend that her back wasn't aching.

*****

For once, Mabel was almost grateful for the holes in her shoes.

They were the same shoes, of course, with which she'd come from the country. Once, they'd been warm and sturdy. Now, London's damp had seeped into the leather, and there was a gap at her left big toe and her right heel. They provided tiny spots of relief as the shoes strained over her swollen feet.

She dragged them across the muddy ground. There were no cobblestones in this part of London. Mud stretched in narrow strips, barely enough to admit a donkey cart, between the buildings that towered on either side. They seemed so huge, these buildings. Their harsh brick walls would dwarf the church spire back home.

Home. Mabel tried not to think of the farm, the hay-scented barn, the fields she'd known down to every stone and clod. She'd worked hard there, terribly hard, yet now she would give anything to exchange the stifling factory for those back-breaking fields.

She pushed the thought aside as she wrapped an arm around her belly, trying to support the weight that dragged at her aching back. There was no time to think of home. She had to think of tomorrow, of what she was going to feed herself and the baby.

She couldn't think too far ahead, though, not to the day that this baby would come. No, no. Only tomorrow. She only had to feed herself tomorrow.

She thought of Josephine, and her heart ached fiercely.

"Stop it, Mabel," she said, turning to one of the ugly brick buildings. Lantern and firelight gleamed through the many holes in the mortar. Paint peeled from its front door, and Mabel had to brace a shoulder against it as she opened it to keep it from swinging on its single hinge.

She pushed it shut and kept her head down, moving quietly down a makeshift hallway. Old sheets, pallets, and scraps of blanket formed partitions between the pitiful tenements. Hers was at the back on the ground floor, a fact that had dismayed her at first, since that floor was so busy and damp. But now, she could only be grateful she didn't have to drag herself up the many flights of rickety stairs.

She pushed a tattered sheet aside—it had cost her precious pennies from a street vendor and the stains would never wash out—and stepped into the place she now called home. There was very little of it. A dirty little fireplace that smoked fiercely stood in the corner opposite the pallet that served as her bed. A cardboard box contained everything she owned, bits and pieces she'd fought to scrounge over the past few months: a cup, a plate, and a saucepan.

She wanted tea. Her dry mouth begged for fluids, but the thought of taking out the pan, going down the street to the pump, and then waiting for the water to heat was too much to bear. The depths of winter were over; she hardly needed a fire to stay alive tonight.

She threw a few bits of coal on the smouldering ashes of yesterday, fell onto the pallet, and wrapped her blanket around herself. The factory had given her tea and rusks twice today and she'd bought a heel of bread on her way home. That would have to do.

"I'm sorry, baby," Mabel whispered.

Exhaustion easily defeated hunger. She was asleep in seconds.

*****

Lightning pain shot through the bottom of Mabel's pelvis. She couldn't bite back the cry as she clasped a hand to her lower abdomen and closed her eyes, riding out the wave of agony.

The women surrounding her edged a step away, terrified to associate themselves with this slacker. Mabel's free hand tightened into a fist on the rags on the table. She struggled to breathe as the pain slowly eased.

Stop it, baby, she thought, blinking back tears. The unborn child squirmed within her; it was as though the little one was dancing on every painful nerve in her back and belly. *You have to stop. You're going to get your mama into trouble.*

"Finch!" Mr. Compton thundered.

Horror swamped her. Mabel straightened, ignoring the pain, and plunged both hands into the horrid mass of rags. Lice swarmed over her arms, sending goosebumps over her skin.

"Finch!" Mr. Compton slammed the cane on the table beside her.

She yelped and flinched away despite herself. Mr. Compton laughed. His cruel eyes found hers as he leaned closer, the smell of cigarette smoke surrounding her.

"What are you doing?" he hissed.

"W-working, sir," Mabel managed.

"It doesn't look like it," Mr. Compton purred. "It looks to me as though you're doing everything but work." He gestured at the pile on the table. "Look at this. You've hardly done what these other girls have—and you're all lazy!"

His voice rose to a crazed yell, and the women yelped.

"I'm sorry, sir," said Mabel. "It's just—" She stopped.

Mr. Compton's eyes narrowed. "Are you making excuses, Finch?"

"No, sir. I'm sorry, sir," Mabel whimpered.

Finch scoffed. He stepped back, glancing again at her belly. "Good, because there are none. Do you understand? There are no excuses here. You do your work and keep up, or you lose your job."

"Yes, sir." The idea clutched at Mabel's heart with a cold hand. Rent was already almost unaffordable. "I'm sorry, sir."

"Catch up to the others," Mr. Compton barked, "or you'll lose half your wage for the day."

The threat was familiar, and it spurred Mabel on despite the pain that blossomed through her belly, or the ache in her feet, or the weakness sucking at her body. It seemed like a hundred years had passed since the bit of rusk and watery tea they were given for breakfast. Mabel tried not to think of how she would savour the gruel they might have for lunch.

She would take each bite slowly, she promised herself as her hands raced over the fabric. She would make it last. Perhaps then the hunger would feel less awful.

The child kicked in her womb again. *I'm sorry, baby,* Mabel thought.

She pushed herself, but her hands refused to work as fast as before. Each time Mr. Compton came around to shout and wave his cane at her, Mabel realized she had fallen further behind. She longed to ask the women around her for help.

That would only get them all into trouble with Mr. Compton.

The shift lasted an eternity. Mabel's feet went from aching to numb. Each time she moved, a fresh pang of pain travelled up her leg and into her belly. She felt her baby twitch and wondered if it hurt the unborn child.

The bell rang at last as Mabel despairingly flung a final handful of rags into the dirty bin. Two full sacks still rested at her feet. She kept her head down as the other women folded up their empty sacks and filed toward the door, each pausing for Mr. Compton to press a few coins into their hands.

Mabel was trembling when she reached the door. She dared not look up and held out a hand, hoping that her palm would be anonymous in the long line of women.

Mr. Compton scoffed. "How many bags do you have left, Finch?"

Mabel dared not look back. "Two, sir." *Please don't ask me to stay and finish them*, she begged him in her heart. It was already ten o' clock; she had to be back at the factory at six.

Mr. Compton's eyes narrowed. Discontented murmurs came from the women behind Mabel as she blocked the door.

"By rights I should make you stay," he said, "but you can't be trusted alone in the factory and I'm not staying up because of a lazy wretch like you. You'll have to work double as fast tomorrow, do you hear me?"

Relief washed through Mabel. Tomorrow would come after glorious sleep. "Yes, sir."

"Very well." Mr. Compton dropped a coin into her hand.

Mabel blinked at it. "Sir…"

"What?" Mr. Compton demanded.

Mabel swallowed. Her usual wages were a sixpence, a penny, and a ha'penny. She didn't know how the numbers worked, but she knew that this wasn't enough. The thruppence sat on her palm, small and lonely despite the crown topping the number 3.

"Did you think you would get paid the same wage as everyone else?" Mr. Compton sneered. "You hardly worked at all, and you cost the company tea and rusks and my time. You can be glad you're getting anything at all, Finch. Now get out of my sight before I take that away, too!"

Mabel clenched her fist over the small coin. "Yes, sir." She tried not to cry. "Sorry, sir."

"Go!" Mr. Compton barked.

Mabel hung her head and joined the listless line of women shuffling to their tenements.

She struggled to calculate how much more money she needed for the rent, but she knew that it was plenty. Monday was only four days away.

She swallowed hard as they passed the dismal market square where bits of bread and dry gruel could be bought. Her body screamed for nourishment, and the musty smell of watery soup reached her from an old woman's cauldron nearby.

But if she didn't have somewhere to live, how would she protect her baby?

Tears gathered in her eyes. She allowed them to flow as she dragged her aching body to the tenement she called home.

Chapter Six

Mabel trembled so fiercely that coins clattered in her hand. Like everyone else in the building at this dreaded time on a Monday morning, she stood at the makeshift door of her tenement, waiting for the landlord to come by.

She doubted that Mr. Stander was actually the building's owner. No, she imagined that the owner was a tycoon of some sort who barely knew that the building and the struggling people within it existed; he merely grew fat on their desperate payments. Mr. Stander was an agent, she guessed, but that made him no less frightening. She had seen him force whole families from their homes before.

The coins clattered again, and Mabel tried to stop her hand from shaking. She had to be brave now, for the baby's sake. There had to be a way for her to reason with this man.

Maybe things would be easier next week. Even as she thought it, Mabel knew she was fooling herself. Her belly was growing bigger, not smaller, and would soon be followed by a small, squalling life utterly dependent on her.

How would she nurse her baby while working? She had seen a few hollow-eyed mothers in the factory. Mr. Compton docked their wages each time they stopped to feed their child. None of them had stayed there long.

A fresh shudder ran through her as voices grew nearer in the gloom. The low, flickering fires and the odd lantern provided the only light. Mr. Stander knew that the people in the tenement were factory workers and he made sure to come by at five on Monday mornings so that no one was at work when he arrived. Mabel could barely make out his stout silhouette, and that only because he was the single fat man in the building. Everyone else had bony shoulders and wild eyes.

He would listen to her if she begged, she thought. She had been a good tenant for the past six months. Maybe if she pleaded, he would give her a few weeks' grace.

Mr. Stander strutted into view. He wore a bowler hat and a strained waistcoat that struggled to contain his belly's curve. His smile was pleasant enough as he doffed his hat to the mother who lived next to Mabel and accepted the usual rate from her—one shilling and ten pennies. She scowled as he moved on.

"Good morning, Mrs. Finch," he said.

"M-Mr. Stander," Mabel croaked.

Mr. Stander held out a hand. "It's been fairer weather lately. Spring's around the corner."

Mabel held her closed hand above his, then hesitated.

"What is it?" Mr. Stander's smile vanished like mist in sunlight.

Mabel bit her lip. "Sir, I'm sorry." She let go of the coins she'd brought—sixpence, five pennies and a ha'penny—and they tinkled into his palm. "I don't have it all yet, sir, but—"

"You know the rules, Mrs. Finch." Mr. Stander met her eyes. "Pay or leave."

Mabel stared at him. How could he be so calm? She had spent the past week surviving only on the scraps given to her at the factory. At that moment, her stomach felt as though it had been violently ripped from her body. Yet this man told her so calmly that it had all been for naught.

"Sir, please," said Mabel, "next week, I'll—"

"The rent is due today. Here. Now." Mr. Stander's smile became fixed. "Pay it or leave. Those are your only choices."

Mabel wrapped an arm around her heavy belly and looked around the building. A few people stared, curious; others looked away. Still others slipped into their tenements in silence. None offered to help her. None extended a hand toward her.

"Please," she whimpered.

"Your pleas are pointless," Mr. Stander snapped. "Do you have the money or not?"

"Sir, my baby's coming soon." Tears rolled down Mabel's cheeks. "I only want somewhere warm and dry to have the little one. I—"

"I asked you a question," Mr. Stander ground out.

Mabel met his eyes and knew that it was true. He didn't care. Just as the entire world had never cared for Mabel, as her brother had chased her from their home, as Ned had cut her out of her inheritance, as Alf and Ada had repelled her from the farm, so too Mr. Stander would never care.

She could do nothing to change his mind.

"No, sir," she said quietly. "I don't have any more money."

"Then you must leave immediately." Mr. Stander pocketed her money and stepped back, then folded his arms. "Are you going to get your things and keep this civil or shall I drag you out?"

"No, sir. I'll leave, sir," Mabel whispered.

She felt numb and distant as she stumbled into her tenement and gathered what she could carry into a cloth bag. It dangled from her hand as she left the tenement and stumbled into the hallway and bumped gently against her leg as she staggered down the makeshift hallway, past the many sets of staring eyes, and into the unforgiving streets of London. Hungry, cold, alone, and now, homeless.

*****

The reality only truly struck her that night when she staggered from the factory.

Mabel stood on the pavement as the other women streamed past her and headed purposefully toward the same buildings that she'd called home only that morning. Now, she had nowhere to go. She wrapped an arm around her belly, trying to relieve her aching back, and stood with her pitiful thruppence in her hand as the other women headed down the street without looking back.

After a few minutes, even Mr. Compton had left without a second glance toward Mabel, and she stood alone. Alone but for the squirming, wriggling child within her. A cold wind struck up from the north—a wind that reminded her summer had not yet fully come—and sliced through her patched and tattered clothing.

The shiver ran through her, and hunger pierced her belly. She looked down at the thruppence in her hand and swallowed. She didn't need it for rent. She might as well try to find a hot meal.

Her aching feet carried her to the market square and a bowl of hot if watery and sour soup from a stringy-haired old woman with a cauldron on a few sticks of wood. Mabel had had the presence of mind to take her tin bowl from the tenement, and she sipped slowly from it as she stood in the square, gazing around.

It felt untethered and strange to be without a home. Not only did Mabel know she would have to sleep outside in the elements, surrounded by danger, but she also felt not quite real somehow. As though not having a home made her not entirely human.

Her body quaked. She took another sip of the soup to calm herself, then tried to focus.

Somewhere warm, she thought. *Out of the wind and rain. Out of the way.*

Her gaze found the deeply recessed doorway of a pawn shop. She stumbled to it and sank down on the steps, clutching her bowl. Her aching feet grew numb with cold as she finished her soup.

People stared, but no one tried to stop her. So she took her blanket from her bag, wrapped it around her body, and tried to sleep.

*****

Agony woke her.

Mabel sat up with a cry as the pain wrenched through her belly. This was very different to the sharp pains when the baby kicked and squirmed or trampled her bladder. This pain gripped her with unrelenting ferocity, tightening the broad dome of her belly, so fierce that darkness swirled before her eyes.

It lasted only a few seconds before releasing her. By then she lay sweating and breathless on the steps, her blanket kicked down to her shins, her back bruised and sore from the way she'd been sleeping.

Gasping for breath, Mabel sat up and gathered her blanket around her shoulders. She clasped both hands over her belly. "What's the matter, baby?" she whispered.

The night was black and silent around her. A single lamppost cast an insufficient yellow glow on the street corner. Mabel's breathing slowed, and she sagged on the steps again, listening as the great church bell struck the half-hour. Half past what? Midnight? Later?

Either way, it wouldn't be long before she had to return to the factory. She needed her rest while she could get it.

Mabel settled on the steps and closed her eyes. It felt as though the lids had barely shut before harsh voices spoke above her head.

"It'll be soon now, won't it?"

"I reckon. She's pretty, too. We'll have a use for her after we've sold it."

Mabel's eyes snapped open. She gasped and scrambled against the door, clutching her blanket, at the sight of the two men standing over her. One was short and skinny; the other had massive arms like tree trunks.

"Leave me alone!" she cried.

The skinny one sighed. "Grab her," he said.

The big one reached for her ankles, but Mabel had farmed with pigs and horses, and defending herself against large animals was nothing new to her. She kicked, hard, and the heel of her boot crunched in his wrist. He lunged back with a yelp and Mabel saw her chance. She scrabbled to her feet, still clinging to her blanket, grabbed her bag and fled.

The church bell tolled five as she bolted across the square. Her shoes slipped and scrabbled on the frosty ground, and panic clutched her chest as she ran, belly bouncing.

"Go on! Get her!" the skinny man yelled.

The big man's feet thudded on cobblestones behind her. Fear made Mabel's breaths come quickly, but she knew she would lose him if she was quick enough.

Crowds of factory workers would soon flow through the district. She had to get away from this deserted marketplace.

Fingers grabbed the back of her dress. Mabel twisted free and dived to the left, plunging down a narrow alley. She heard a grunt of surprise behind her as she sprinted behind the homes, arms wrapped around her belly to support it. There was an open door on her right; she didn't know where it led, only saw the dark gap and flung herself through it.

Mabel's feet tangled in straw, and she fell painfully on her knees. A stable, she realized, smelling manure. She was in a stable with no windows.

There was no way out, and she heard the thump of feet in the alley.

Mabel crawled beneath the stone manger in the corner, curled up tight, and tried to breathe quietly. The footsteps went straight past the stable, but she dared not move. What if he turned around and came back?

The next pain caught her unawares, and she nearly screamed. She cupped her hand over her mouth to silence herself as a wave of agony rocked her, squeezing her belly and pelvis. Tears rolled from her closed eyes as she clung on through the pain. In that moment, if he had crashed into the room, Mabel would hardly had noticed. Her world was nothing but pain.

Slowly, slowly, it faded, and Mabel opened her eyes. The stable was empty and she heard no sounds of pursuit outside.

For a few moments, she lay, panting and scared, in the straw. Then she dragged herself to her feet.

It was time to get to work.

*****

The pains were coming quicker now.

This one doubled Mabel over at the rag table. She didn't want to react, but she had no choice; staying upright was impossible. Her hands tightened around the rags, squeezing panicked lice between her fingers, and her quaking knees almost gave way. Her elbows slammed against the wood and she ground her teeth to keep from screaming.

The women around her gave her wide-eyed looks, but no one dared to ask.

The pain lasted longer this time. It lasted longer every time, and they were coming on more and more frequently. She was sweating and breathless, her ears ringing, when it finally eased.

"Finch—" Mr. Compton began.

The bell's ring cut him off. The torturous shift was finally over; Mabel felt a hint of surprise that she had survived.

He scowled, then took his position at the door. The women shuffled past, accepting their tiny wages. Mabel clasped both hands to her belly and breathed hard, aware of sweat trickling down her back despite the chilly air.

When she reached the door, Mr. Compton sneered and flicked the customary thruppence in her direction. She took it numbly and stumbled out of the factory, hardly caring. She wasn't hungry. Everything hurt too much.

She was barely out of the factory door, the cold air strangely blissful, when another pain seized her. A scream wrenched from her lips. She grabbed the lamppost and doubled over, trying to breathe in desperate gulps as her head spun and panic clutched her.

I'm sorry, baby, Mabel wept inwardly. *I'm so sorry.* She didn't know what was going wrong with her poor unborn child, but it had to be something truly terrible for this pain to swamp her. Terror and dismay washed over her like a tidal wave. What if her poor child didn't make it?

Something wet and warm gushed over her thighs as the pain ebbed. Mabel blinked down, startled, at the dark pool spreading between her shoes. People flinched and cried out around her, disgusted, but she knew suddenly that it wasn't what they thought.

No one had ever told Mabel much about how babies came into the world, but she was a farmer's wife. She'd helped to birth piglets and calves, and she knew what this fluid was.

My baby is coming. My baby is coming!

The thought brought an indescribable mix of joy and terror to her heart. The joy almost frightened her more than anything else. She realized suddenly how long she had been yearning to hold this tiny human being in her arms.

Then the terror crushed her. She was on the street, alone. How was she going to deliver this baby? How was she going to keep her child alive?

She whirled around and almost collided with another of the factory women. Janet. She stood opposite Mabel at the rag table.

"Janet, help me," Mabel cried, grabbing her sleeves. "Please. I'm having my baby. I need help."

Janet's eyes widened in horror. She shook Mabel's arms away and hurried off.

Mabel turned, disoriented in the crush of women leaving the factory, and spotted another colleague. "Bertha," she cried, limping toward her. "Please, Bertha, my baby's coming. Please help me."

The woman ducked her head as though Mabel was invisible and rushed away.

Panic gripped her.

"Someone, please help me," Mabel cried out, her voice ringing around the street. "I'm having my baby. I need help!"

Her cry echoed from one pitiless factory wall to the other, and the street magically emptied, everyone present fleeing from her cry for help.

As always, Mabel was alone.

Chapter Seven

Mabel panted through the end of the pain, and sudden clarity filled her mind as she stared at the deserted street. She was alone; she was always alone. No one was going to help her, but there was no stopping what was happening now. She was having this baby and she was going to have to do it on her own.

No use pitying herself. No use trying to get help.

She thought frantically of what she did for the sows and cattle when their young came. Clean, dry straw. A warm place out of the wind. She'd have to do her best to find something along those lines.

Her gaze rested on an alley between two of the less disgusting warehouses. They contained only fabric and paper, none of the toxic rubbish from the other factories, and Mabel made for it as quickly as she could. She felt the first tendrils of another pain spreading over her abdomen by the time she reached the alley and frantically plucked her blanket from her bag. It was the best she could do, but her heart screamed at the injustice as she spread the grubby blanket on the ground.

Smeared with dirt and streaked with dust, it was still cleaner than the alley floor.

Now she needed to construct a makeshift shelter. The two walls protected her from much of the wind, but a chill still came from—

The next pain dropped her to her hands and knees. A guttural scream wrenched from her as agony flooded her body. Her back and belly contracted with such strength that the muscles felt as though they would rip themselves from her bones. Her sodden petticoats cooled and clung to her, and she shivered as the pain faded, leaving only terrible cold.

"I'm sorry," Mabel sobbed, tears pouring down her cheeks. "My poor baby. Born in an alley. I'm so sorry. I'm so, so sorry."

She sagged onto her side and curled up, breathing hard, waiting for the next pain. How long did it take? How would her baby come out? Front limbs first, like a calf? She didn't know. She wouldn't know if something went wrong, either.

What if she lost her poor baby?

"I'm sorry," Mabel whimpered. "I'm so sorry."

The relentless progression of labour left her only a few minutes of rest. She had just begun to drop off to sleep when the next pain seized her, making her curl up, knees to chest. Pressure crushed her pelvis and her scream rang around the walls, fading to sobs as the pain finally passed.

She lay on her side, breathing hard, knees apart in a bid to relieve the steady waves of agony that now pulsed through her even between birthing pains. Her hands clasped her belly.

Did she feel the baby move, or was that her own body shaking? When last had she felt the baby stir? Was her baby still alive?

Quiet dismay overwhelmed her as she let her head rest on the blanket. "I'm sorry, baby," she moaned. She couldn't wait to see and hold her child, but not like this. Oh, not like this! How would she survive another pain? Would there be many more? When they were over... what then?

Utter despair washed over her. She thought of the little church in the village back home and realized she had nowhere else to turn, nowhere at all.

Oh, God, she prayed. *Help me!*

The tiny, desperate prayer was all she had time for as another pain racked her. This one seemed to last an eternity, longer than her scream. Sweating, chest heaving, Mabel lay limp against her blanket. Dizziness swirled in her vision. *How many more?* she wondered. *How will I make it?*

"Hello!" a voice called.

Mabel blinked, thinking she was imagining things. She focused on breathing and preparing for another pain.

"Hello! Hi! Can you hear me?" Tentative footsteps approached.

Nausea rolled in Mabel's gut as she forced herself to sit up and cried out at the pressure. What if someone was about to attack her? Could she run? She didn't think so.

"Do you need help?" the voice called.

Mabel turned toward it, then blinked at a silhouette in the dark. A woman's silhouette. She stood a few yards away, hesitant.

"I heard you cry out," the woman said. "I thought perhaps you needed something. What's your name?"

The syllables escaped over her chapped lips. "Mabel."

"Hello, Mabel. Are you all right?" the stranger asked.

Mabel hardly knew what to say. Was this stranger being kind? Did she mean any harm? It was so hard to tell, and she felt another pain building in her muscles.

"Polly!" someone called.

"Charlie, come here!" Polly shouted back. "Somebody needs help."

Footsteps approached at the top of the alley. Mabel shrank back, terrified.

"It's all right. It's only my brother. Do you need help, Mabel?" Polly asked.

The word slipped from Mabel before she could stop it. "Yes," she sobbed.

"All right. Hold on, let me strike a match," said Polly.

There was a moment's rummaging in pockets and suddenly a small flame flared. Mabel looked up into the face of an angel. Golden ringlets surrounded smooth, pale cheeks, and the eyes were large and green, ringed with thick lashes and gentle concern.

"Oh," Polly gasped. "Oh, you're—you're—"

The next pain seized Mabel, flinging her down on the blanket. She writhed, moaning, aware of nothing except the agony. Then there came something else: a touch, a human touch, something she hadn't felt in a long time. Cool fingers closed around hers and squeezed. She squeezed back as the pain slowly left her.

"You're having a baby, aren't you?" said Polly.

"Help me," Mabel cried. "Help me. Please. Please!"

"Polly—" a masculine voice began.

"Pick her up, Charlie," Polly ordered, her voice offering no alternative. "We need to get her home." She squeezed Mabel's hand lightly as strong arms lifted her. "Don't worry about a thing, Mabel. I'm here. We're going to help you."

Mabel closed her eyes as she felt herself being carried from the alley. Weakness, pain and shock swirled through her, making Polly's voice seem very far away. Perhaps she was dying, she thought. Perhaps these were angels carrying her to heaven.

*****

The place to which Charlie and Polly bore her was as much like heaven as Mabel supposed she could hope for. She found herself lying on a clean bed, one that was twice the width of her pallet in the tenement, with clean sheets surrounding her. Candles sputtered in their niches and a great fire in the corner provided golden warmth. Polly bustled back and forth, draping towels over a rail by the fire, bringing cups of water to Mabel.

She would have been convinced that this was heaven, in fact, if it wasn't for the pains. They came on harder and faster now, and the pressure had become unbearable.

Mabel tried to grit her teeth over a scream as another pain gripped her. It squeezed and squeezed until she couldn't breathe, until she felt her heart would burst. The scream spilled from her, guttural and terrified.

"That's it, dear," said Polly. She crouched at the foot of the bed, peering between Mabel's knees. "That's it! One more! One more big one. Your baby's nearly here!"

The pain left her. Mabel collapsed on the bed, drenched in sweat, gasping for breath. Weakness made her muscles feel like the wads of half-boiled rags that eventually became paper: limp and colourless.

"I can't," she sobbed. "I can't do it."

"Yes you can, dear, and you will!" Poppy gripped Mabel's shin with a bloodied hand. "You'll do this for your baby. It's nearly here. You're about to hold it in your arms at last."

The thought sent strength surging through Mabel. Another pain seized her, and this time, Mabel didn't try to fight it. She allowed her back to curl and screamed with determination, and then suddenly, blissfully, it was over.

Polly scrambled to her feet and wrapped a bloodied bundle in warm towels.

"Is my baby breathing?" Mabel gasped, sweat cooling on her skin. "Is my baby alive?"

Polly rubbed furiously with a towel. "Come on, baby. Come on. Come—"

Then the most glorious sound in the world split the night: the feeble cry of tiny lungs taking their first breath.

Polly raised her head, tears sparkling on her cheeks. "It's a boy, Mabel," she said. "It's a beautiful little boy."

She held out the towel-wrapped bundle to Mabel, who took it eagerly and laid her baby boy on her chest for the first time. Suddenly all weakness had left her arms. She could take and hold her child with hands that did not tremble.

She looked down into the face of her child, still smeared with fluids, screwed up in a toothless yell, blotched red and purple with the effort of birth.

It was the most splendid thing she had ever seen, and in that instant, everything changed.

*****

Sunlight.

It played on Mabel's closed eyelids, warm and welcoming on her clean skin. A pillow cushioned her head, and when she gently stirred her sleepy limbs, she felt something that had eluded her for six months.

Comfort.

It wasn't perfect comfort, of course. Her body ached ferociously in many different ways. Yet she knew that clean sheets were wrapped around her and that she rested on a mattress stuffed with springy straw.

She exhaled and her arms tightened around the tiny, warm bundle sharing her pillow.

Her baby.

Mabel's eyes opened slowly, and for a few moments, she could do nothing but stare in awe at her beautiful child. Now that he was clean and dry with a little makeshift knitted cap on his head, her baby was lovelier than ever. His skin was peachy pink and his long, pale eyelashes swept his cheek as he slept.

"Hello, little one," Mabel whispered.

A chair creaked behind her. "You're awake," said Polly.

Mabel had thought she was dreaming. Perhaps she was still dreaming. She gathered her baby in her arms and sat up, staring around the room. It had been nothing but a vague blur the day before, but now she saw that the wallpaper was clean if old and faded, that the creaky floorboards had recently been scrubbed, and that the oft-mended curtains hung softly over a window filled with sunlight.

She couldn't remember if she had ever been asleep while the sun shone before.

Polly sat in a rocking chair beside the bed. It squeaked with protest each time she moved. Her eyes were sky blue and the ringlets surrounding her face were brighter than ever in the sunlight.

"You... who are you?" Mabel whispered. "Are you an angel?"

Polly gave a gentle laugh. "An angel! Bless your heart, dear, no. Not even in the slightest." She laughed again.

"Then why did you help me?" Mabel asked.

Polly rested a hand on Mabel's arm. "Because you needed help and we were in the position to give it. Who wouldn't?"

Her eyes seemed genuinely surprised that Mabel thought any alternatives were possible. Tears stung Mabel's as she thought of the dozens of people who'd passed her as she laboured in an alley. Now, she was in a clean, warm bed. Someone had washed her baby and tucked him snugly into her arms.

That someone was the sweet, smiling girl sitting beside her. Polly looked even younger than Mabel, she guessed. Eighteen, perhaps, no older.

"Thank you," Mabel croaked. The words could never be adequate.

"Would you like some tea?" Polly asked.

Mabel blinked rapidly. "I'll—I'll make it."

"Nonsense, dear. You need rest," said Polly firmly. "I'll make it and then we'll talk."

She returned a few minutes later with tin mugs and a chipped porcelain teapot whose decorations had long since faded. Polly raised it with obvious pride and poured delicately into the tin mugs, then added generous amounts of sugar and a drop of milk before holding it to Mabel.

Her arms tightened around the baby, who whimpered in protest. "What if I spill and burn him?" Mabel whispered.

Polly smiled. "Don't worry. You won't, and I've made it hardly lukewarm, dear."

"You think of everything," Mabel admitted. She took the mug and raised it to her lips, then drained it in moments; she was thirstier than she'd realized.

"Sorry," she said, handing back the empty mug.

"Don't worry, dear. There's plenty," said Polly.

She poured another mug of tea; it was weak, but Mabel drank it more slowly this time, savouring every sip. A knot of fear gathered at the top of her stomach as she did so. The comfortable bed, the friendly girl, the sweet tea—it was all far too good to be true. In minutes, she would be told to get out, or shown what she owed them for their kindness. What if they wanted money? Mabel had had thruppence, but she no longer wore the filthy dress where she'd stashed it. Where had it gone? It surely wouldn't be enough. Had she ruined any sheets?

Heart pounding, she hugged her baby to her chest. What if they wanted to take her son?

"You look frightened, Mabel," said Polly gently. "What's the matter?"

"I—I don't have money," Mabel cried. "I hope I can still work at the factory. Mr. Compton is so cruel, and—and—" Tears spilled over.

"Now, now, don't cry. There are plenty of jobs in this city," said Polly. She rested a hand on Mabel's knee. "Why don't you start at the beginning and tell me everything?"

The question dried Mabel's tears instantly. No one had ever asked her that before, and it opened a door she hadn't known she'd shut. The truth poured out of her before she could stop it. She told her everything, from the pox outbreak that took her parents, to Ned's cruelty and death, to Alf and Ada and the factory.

Polly listened in silence the entire time, nodding at intervals. She only spoke when Mabel was finished.

"You poor, poor thing," she said. "How much sorrow you've had! But look." She smiled and touched the baby's swaddled feet. "Look at the wonderful joy you've been given."

Mabel gazed down at her child. She knew that she would have to feed him now when she had barely been able to feed herself; she knew that life was hard and that it would be almost impossible for this baby. But none of that could crush the sheer, overwhelming pleasure that she felt when she looked at his sleeping face. The terribleness of the world could never drown out the utter wonder of holding her child in her arms.

"He's perfect," she whispered.

"Of course he is," said Polly. "Do you have a name picked out for him yet?"

Mabel traced the line of her baby's plump cheek with her forefinger. "I suppose I should name him Edgar after his father."

"I suppose," said Polly, "that Edgar was rather horrible, and you should name him whatever you like. What about John? It's a lovely name. It's from the Bible."

"John," Mabel murmured. "It is a nice name, but..." She paused, then smiled. "You know the story of Jack and the Beanstalk, don't you?"

Polly laughed. "The fairytale? Of course."

"I always thought that Jack was a great hero. He made mistakes, of course. But he started out with nothing, and he ended with killing giants." Mabel smiled. "It's short for John, too."

"That's right," said Polly.

"Then I think that's what I'll name my little boy." Mabel bent and kissed the impossible smoothness of his forehead. "Jack Finch. He'll be my little Jack."

*****

Mabel was well enough to move around by the next day. Polly asked a neighbour—an equally friendly, plump older woman—to show Mabel how to swaddle little Jack on her chest with a length of cloth Polly gave her, and the baby nestled happily against his mother, sucking his tiny thumb and sleeping as she came slowly downstairs.

It was still dark. Polly had to be at work by six, as Mabel always used to do, too. It was just past five now, but the tiny kitchen in the little cottage already smelled of toast. Polly bustled around by a cast-iron stove and a young man sat at the little round table, which was only really big enough for two, pushed up against the small window overlooking the smithy.

"Good morning," said Mabel shyly.

The young man looked up. "Mabel!" he said, springing to his feet. He blushed. "You look much better."

"She wasn't ill, Charlie, silly." Polly laughed. "She was having a baby."

"Yes, well." Charlie blushed more deeply. His round, boyish cheeks turned tomato red beneath a mop of straw-coloured hair so much like his sisters.

"You carried me here," said Mabel. "Thank you. Thank you so very much. Jack and I wouldn't have lived if not for you."

Charlie met her gaze. He had deep brown eyes as friendly as a puppy's. "Polly loves to help people. I love to help Polly. Maybe I'm learning her ways." He smiled.

Mabel returned it. "How can I help, Polly?"

"You can have a seat." Polly set a sliced loaf of bread, each slice bearing a thin layer of butter, on the table. "Breakfast's all ready."

Charlie pulled out a chair and stepped back, gesturing to it.

"I'll sit on the stool." Mabel inclined her head toward the three-legged stool by the stove.

"Please, don't be ridiculous. I'll take the stool," said Charlie.

He perched on it and Mabel took a seat at the table. Polly piled a tin plate with slices of bread and pushed it toward her.

"I couldn't," said Mabel.

"You certainly could," said Polly. "Charlie's just gotten a raise from the blacksmith. He's getting really good at shoeing them horses." She smiled. "We can feed you for a few days, dear. Don't fret."

Mabel took the plate and stared at it. The few slices of bread were more food than she'd eaten in one meal since Ned's death. Sudden tears stung her eyes. She cupped a hand around the back of Jack's head and tried to hold them back, but they spilled down her cheeks in any case.

"Now, now," said Polly. "No need for that, dear."

"I'll go back to the factory tomorrow," Mabel promised. "I'll go and beg for my job. I'll take Jack with me, swaddled like this, and I'll work and I'll find another tenement, I will. Thank you. Thank you."

"There's no need to find another tenement," said Polly firmly. "We can share our room, you and me. I'm tired of being all on my own anyway. And we need another pair of hands around the house."

This latest generosity drew a great flood of tears from Mabel. Unable to hold it back, she covered her face with her hands and wept.

"Hush, dear. Hush. Eat your breakfast," said Polly.

"Let her cry, Polly," said Charlie softly. He rested a hand on Mabel's arm; it was hard and callused, but the touch was gentle. She found the courage to raise her eyes to his, and their brown warmth smiled right into the pit of her soul.

Part Three

Chapter Eight

Four Years Later

Mabel drew a knitted scarf tight around her neck against the wintry chill. The wool had been cheap and was rough against her skin, but the close stitches still blocked the cold breeze that howled down the dark street, bringing a fistful of sleet with it.

"Brrrr!" said Polly beside her. "I don't think the world has realized it's spring yet."

Mabel laughed. It was so easy to do with Polly by her side. Despite her own long shift at the cotton mill, Polly's blue eyes sparkled, and she smiled up at Mabel. "Long day?" she asked.

Mabel nodded. "Mr. Compton hasn't forgiven me for coming back after I vanished to have Jack, you know. He still treats me worse than all the other women. But at least he paid me a full wage today."

"What a silly old goat he is." Polly chuckled. "I had to laugh at Mr. Jones today, too. He gets *so* worked up over the silliest things. I was quite scared of him when I was a piecer as a girl, but now, as a weaver, I think he's quite ridiculous. Imagine getting so bothered over something so silly!"

She laughed, and Mabel joined in again despite the louse bites on her hands and the exhaustion throbbing through her limbs as they walked the single block toward home.

"Can you believe it's been four years?" Polly murmured.

Mabel shook her head. "It feels like yesterday, but also a lifetime ago."

They both stared down the black alley where Mabel had laboured alone in the cold.

"You saved our lives that day," said Mabel.

"Oh, Mabel, dear, as if you and Jack haven't made ours a thousand times better, too." Polly beamed as she threaded her arm through Mabel's. "Come on, now. I think we should make some fish for supper, don't you? Before it goes bad."

They rounded the block, and then the cottage lay like a happy oasis amid the looming warehouses surrounding them.

A streetlamp cast a friendly yellow light on the long, squat building that housed the smithy. Great metal gates on one side guarded the entrance to the shop where customers could lead their horses inside for shoeing. The large space allowed two smiths to work at the same time. On the other side, a little strip of garden—dead and still now, so early in spring—guarded the two-bedroom cottage. Its shuttered windows looked like sleepy eyes. Chinks of light spilled between them.

The old blacksmith had once lived in this cottage, but as London grew up around him and his smithy grew busier and busier, he had found himself able to buy a nicer house in a better part of town. Charlie and Polly lived in the cottage to service late customers, which were common given the factories' long hours. A lost shoe on a horse transporting goods to the docks could mean a great loss in profit. Owners were happy to pay a premium to these smiths, the only ones in the area.

Perhaps that was why they were able to afford meat for dinner almost every night, even though Mabel knew full well that the blacksmith took more than the lion's share of the money.

The front door crashed open as Polly and Mabel approached. "Mama!" a little voice called.

This was the most glorious part of Mabel's day. Her face erupted into a smile as she rushed forward and held out her arms. A little figure sprinted from the open door, giggling, and ran across the cobbled street toward her.

In the streetlamp's glow, Jack was the most beautiful thing Mabel had ever seen. His soft brown curls, so much like hers, bounced on his shoulders. Friendly green eyes beamed up at her as she scooped him into her arms and swung him around. The music of his laughter filled her ears, and she hugged him close to her, feeling the steady flutter of his heartbeat. He wrapped his arms around her neck and pulled her close.

"Hello, Jack-Jack," Mabel murmured, kissing his cheek.

"Mama." Jack sighed with pleasure and tucked his head under her chin.

"I'm here too, you little rascal." Polly grabbed the boy's foot and wiggled it.

"Auntie Polly!" Jack held out his arms to her.

Polly took him and gave him a squeeze. A sudden, wet cough escaped her. She bent down and put Jack on his feet, then coughed again.

"You all right there, Polly?" Charlie asked from the doorway. Concern flooded his face as he hurried from the cottage.

"Oh, Charlie, don't be such a mother hen," said Polly hoarsely. "Just got something in my throat, that's all. Now let's get inside. I've had about enough of these streets."

She bustled into the cottage, and Jack hurried after her, clinging to her skirt. That left Mabel and Charlie outside on the pavement, the streetlight making his brown eyes deeper than ever, its yellow glow playing over his hair and turning it to gold.

"How was your day?" he murmured.

Mabel stepped a little closer. Not close enough to be improper, but so close that she could smell his unique aroma of metal and fire. "Long and hard," she said, "but it's over now."

"It is indeed." Charlie reached up and brushed her shoulder with his fingertips, then let his hand fall to his side. She felt warm lines throb on her skin where he'd touched her. "Now you're here with the people who care about you."

"The people I care about, too," Mabel said softly.

He smiled, filling her heart. "I wanted to ask you something."

Now? Mabel thought. *Finally, after four long years*. Her pulse raced. "What?" she asked breathlessly.

Charlie blushed, a charmingly dark hue. "I, ah, I've been saving. I bought two tickets to the music hall down the street. They say there's a little band playing there on Sunday after church. Polly says she'll stay home with Jack, if—" He stopped. "If you want to come with me."

Excitement flipped in Mabel's chest. "Oh, Charlie," she whispered.

"If you'd like that," said Charlie.

She didn't know what to say that wouldn't fluster him even more, so she simply smiled and said, "I would love that."

They turned and went into the cottage together.

*****

Mabel couldn't remember the last time she'd heard music outside of a church. And though she loved the sombre notes of the organ that towered above listeners' heads in the small church they attended, it felt like a different world to hear a fiddle again.

She and Charlie had taken the ha'penny spots uncomfortably close to the stage. They perched on hard, uncomfortable wooden benches and had to crane their necks to see the performers on the splinter-ridden stage.

There were two men with fiddles and one with the piano, and they scraped out a merry and enthusiastic tune so cheerful that it was easy to forgive the odd wrong note.

The woman with them was skinny, but her voice belied her small figure. Its power rolled through the music hall as she sang.

"Jocky met with Jenny fair

Aft by the dawning of the day

But Jocky is now fu' of care

Since Jenny stole his heart away."

Feet tapped through the music hall, and Mabel allowed hers to join in. Beside her, Charlie grinned and clapped his hands to the beat. She did the same, and soon the entire music hall was clapping and stamping along with the singer as she rollicked through the song.

The singer repeated the last refrain twice before the song ended with a flourishing piano riff. The hall erupted into applause. Red-cheeked from stamping and clapping, Mabel laughed along with Charlie as they joined in.

The night air was cold when they emerged from the hall, but Charlie's presence by her side felt as warm as a hearth fire. He walked very close beside her as they began their stroll home through the gathering evening. For once, London was beautiful. It was a clear day, the sunlight soft and forgiving on the buildings' brick facades, calling Mabel's attention to the tiny wildflowers struggling between the cobblestones and the beauty of a stray ginger cat sleeping on a wall, its paws tucked beneath its chin.

Charlie's hand brushed against the back of hers. She opened her fingers almost without thinking, and his hand interlaced with hers, then squeezed softly. How was it possible for his fingers to be so warm?

"Thank you," she said shyly. "That was really nice. No one's ever done anything like that for me before."

Charlie smiled. "I can't believe that. Your former husband must have been a real beast not to spoil you with everything you could possibly want."

His words made her blush like a schoolgirl, and she giggled. His hand tightened on hers like he was afraid she'd pull away.

"I've never been so happy in my life," he murmured. "I have been content to share a home with Polly. Lucky for me she never married, she's been a wonderful sister to me, though, taking care of me all these years. Although she probably doesn't see it that way," Charlie chuckled.

"I agree, Polly is wonderful," said Mabel.

"She is." Charlie's face lit up. "I've never met someone so good and kind. It seems as though she's never thought even a bad thought about another person. All she does is good things. In a world of bad, it's an uncommon thing. I'm glad she is my family."

A strange pang of jealousy pierced Mabel's belly, but she shoved it away for its foolishness. "She does do good, uncommon good."

"Then we found you." Charlie gazed down at her, his eyes large and bright. "And dear Jack-Jack, and everything got even better."

He fell silent, and Mabel was happy to walk with him in quiet, hand in his. Their footpath approached a narrow, humpbacked bridge over a tributary of the Thames. This one flowed toward the factories, not away from them, and had not yet been polluted. Its waters were brown but did not reek as they splashed quietly between the banks. Spring grass and dandelions had begun to bloom beneath the stones of the old bridge.

Charlie stopped suddenly at the peak of the bridge. His hand quivered on hers.

"Charlie?" said Mabel. "Is everything all right?"

Charlie took a deep breath. His cheeks glowed, but there was determination in his eyes.

"I've never seen Polly so happy as she is having a friend like you," he said softly. "I've never known our cottage so full of laughter."

The kind words brought a blush to Mabel's cheeks. "For my part," she said quietly, "I didn't know that it was possible to live with people who were kind and gentle like you and Polly are."

Charlie's eyes widened. Something changed within them, as though what Mabel said had changed his mind—or perhaps made his mind up.

He squared his shoulders and turned to face her. He held out his other hand, and Mabel laid her fingers in his before she could think about it.

A cool breeze blew in over the river. It brought with it the scents of a different place, somewhere far from this polluted city; it smelled, just for a moment and just for a little, like the farm's fields in the springtime. Looking into his eyes reminded Mabel that there was more to the world than London and its cruelties.

Charlie sank.

"Are you all right?" Mabel cried, gripping his hands.

"I'm quite all right," Charlie managed, his voice cracking. He released her hand to reach into his pocket as he lowered himself to one knee.

"Charlie, get up," said Mabel. "What happened? Did you slip?"

"No, my dear." Charlie laughed. "I didn't."

He drew forth a small round object from his pocket—a ring, Mabel realized. It was made of iron; she could clearly see the hammer marks where he'd pounded it into shape.

"Mabel Finch," Charlie whispered, "you make me so happy. Will you marry me?"

Mabel gasped. She snatched her hands to her mouth, her heart pounding wildly. How had this happened so quickly? And yet, looking back over the past four years, she felt that maybe it hadn't happened quickly enough.

He was kind and good. She could never imagine him striking or cursing her, and Jack loved him like the father he'd never had. The stepfather he could have now.

"Yes!" Mabel burst out. "Yes, I'll marry you!"

Charlie's face split into a wide grin. He bounded to his feet as he slipped the ring over her finger. It was a perfect fit.

"How could it fit so well?" Mabel wondered, raising her hand to admire the simple iron loop on her digit. Ned had never bothered with things like rings.

"Polly helped," said Charlie, "like she always does."

Mabel laughed. She looked up at Charlie, at her new fiancé, and that crisp wind came again. It tasted of a new life, of a future; one doubtlessly filled with hard work, but also with promise.

He might become the blacksmith someday and own the entire smithy. Then she would never have to work in a factory again. She and Polly could stay at home, doing mending or looking after children perhaps, and Jack would grow up with his mother by his side.

Happy tears spilled over her cheeks.

"Mabel?" said Charlie, alarmed.

"Thank you, Charlie," said Mabel. She gripped his hands tightly. "Thank you!"

Chapter Nine

Newspaper rustled in Polly's hands as she and Mabel walked together through the dark streets. They joined a steady stream of pale, grubby people who moved as quietly and stiffly as reanimated corpses, heading toward the factories and the work waiting within.

For once, Mabel hardly cared. She was smiling as she strolled beside Polly.

"Just look at it," Polly breathed. "Isn't it wonderful?"

"May I see it one more time?" Mabel asked.

"Of course you can, dear." Polly paused beneath a streetlamp, ignoring frowns from their fellow workers as they dodged around them. "It's yours, isn't it?"

Mabel squinted at the tight rows of print that seemed far too close together. She could make out letters here and there, but nothing more; Polly had tried to show her how to read but there simply wasn't time.

"There," said Polly patiently. She pointed.

Mabel could just about see the shape of her name, *Mabel Finch*. She was learning to recognize Charlie's as well, written right beside hers: *Charles Wilson*.

"*Charles Wilson announces his engagement to Mabel Finch*," Polly read out loud. "Now isn't that lovely!"

"It must have cost so much money for him to put it in the paper," said Mabel.

"Don't you worry about that, dear. He wanted to do it. He's so proud of you. He couldn't wait to see your two names together." Polly beamed. "He'll do it again after the wedding."

"Ash." Mabel sighed with happy excitement. "The wedding."

Polly folded the paper and tucked it inside her coat. They kept walking, rejoining the shuffling mass of workers, but Mabel felt as though they stood out today. Happiness burned in her chest like a candle flame.

"I know you've been married before, but I'm sure you're still excited," said Polly.

"I never had a real wedding," said Mabel. "We went to the church alone; the vicar's wife and son were our witnesses. We said some vows and went home. That was it."

"Well, that Ned was good for nothing, so I'm hardly surprised," said Polly vehemently. "This time will be different, dear. We'll have—" She stopped and pressed a hand to her chest.

"Are you all right, Polly?" Mabel asked.

Polly erupted into a fit of coughing. They were horrible coughs, deep and chesty, and sounded like ripping flesh.

"Polly!" Mabel cried.

Polly held up a hand as she coughed into her sleeve. Around them, the pavement cleared magically, everyone giving them a wide berth.

"Polly, I'll get help." Mabel looked around wildly.

"No, no, dear," Polly rasped. "It's all right." She straightened, wiping her mouth. Was that a smear of blood on her sleeve?

"You're not all right." Mabel seized her arm. "You're sick."

"Not at all. Don't worry yourself so, Mabel. It's not good for you." Polly gave a cheerful smile as she straightened her dress. "Now, let's talk about the wedding! What do you think, blue or green for your new dress?"

Mabel rubbed her chin. "I think green is best."

"It really is. It brings out your eyes." Polly smiled. "It might not be a white dress like the rich folk can wear, but you'll wear it every day for years, and each time you put it on you'll think of your wedding."

The thought made Mabel smile. "That's lovely, Polly. Thank you."

"As for flowers, well, you've chosen a good time of year," said Polly.

Mabel blushed. "I would love flowers at our wedding, but surely they'll be much too expensive, Polly."

"Not at all. That's what I was saying," said Polly. "It's almost summer, you know. Jack and I can go scavenging in the hedgerows and parks. I'm sure we'll find a beautiful bouquet for you and a buttonhole for dear Charlie... too." She seemed breathless, beads of sweat gathering on her upper lip.

"Are you sure you're all right?" Mabel asked as they approached the crossroads where they would go different ways; she left to the rag factory, Polly right to the cotton mill.

"Quite all right, dear," said Polly faintly. Her breath rattled in her throat. "Don't you worry. Everything... is quite... all right."

She stopped, and her knees buckled.

"Polly!" Mabel cried.

She lunged to catch the crumpling girl, throwing her arms around Polly's shoulders before her head could meet the pavement. Her heart fluttered in her neck and elbows as she tried to make Polly sit up against the nearest wall, but she was as limp as a rag doll. She crumpled to the grimy pavement, golden curls spilling against filthy cobblestones. Her face was almost translucent against the warm tones of her hair. A blue line surrounded her lips.

"Polly!" Mabel screamed. "Polly, wake up!"

She shook her shoulders and gently tapped her face, but Polly didn't stir. Her chest moved faintly, dragging ragged gasps of air through her open mouth.

"Please, Polly, wake up," Mabel begged.

She shook her again, and Polly's eyelids fluttered. She coughed, hard, and blood sprayed on the cobblestones.

"No," Mabel gasped.

"M-Mae," Polly croaked.

Mabel fought to calm her racing heart. "It's all right, Polly," she said. "Lie still. Don't try to talk. I—I'm going to find help. Stay right here. I'll find help."

Polly nodded and closed her eyes, which in itself terrified Mabel. The Polly she knew would have bounced to her feet and ordered Mabel to stop being silly.

She took her future sister-in-law's purse from her pocket to keep it from being stolen, then turned and sprinted down the street. Still a block away, she started screaming Charlie's name.

*****

Half the wedding dress money went to the doctor, but Mabel didn't care. She would have given him the flesh from her bones if that was what he needed.

She stood very quietly in the corner of the room—the same room where Jack had been born—and wrung her hands. Polly lay on her side in the clean bed, her loose hair sprayed on the pillow, her eyes closed. Her chest seemed to be barely moving as the old doctor struggled to bend over her. His joints creaked audibly as he moved a thin wooden funnel across her chest, holding his ear to the pointed end at intervals.

Dr. Cradock had seen Jack once or twice, too, and Mabel thought she understood his expressions. Her heart froze when he straightened slowly, back creaking, and turned to her.

His thin mouth was turned down at the edges, wrinkling the white stubble around his lips.

"Rest now, Miss Wilson," he said, laying a fatherly hand on Polly's shoulder. "The medicine will help you sleep."

"Thank you, doctor," Polly mumbled.

Her eyes closed, and her breaths fell into a slow rhythm. Dr. Cradock stepped back and Mabel hurried in, to tuck Polly under the covers. She added their extra blanket from under the bed and pulled it all up to her chin. Polly's skin felt so terribly cold. Her breathing held a steady wheeze that clutched at Mabel's heart with icy claws.

Dr. Cradock motioned for her to go ahead, and she stepped out of the bedroom. Charlie had been sitting at the kitchen table. He shot to his feet now, clutching his cloth cap in his hands, his face streaked with soot from working in the smithy. His eyes were huge and round and terrified.

"What's the matter with her, doctor?" he cried.

Dr. Cradock shut the bedroom door quietly behind them.

"I think you should all sit down," he said softly.

Mabel's knees turned to water. She put the kettle on the stove, desperate for her hands to do something, and Charlie sagged onto his stool.

"It's bad news, then," he said.

Mabel's hands shook so hard that water slopped from the kettle onto the hot cast iron and sizzled.

"I'm sorry, Mr. Wilson," said Dr. Cradock. "I'm afraid that it is very bad news."

Mabel turned toward him, her hands tangled in her skirt now. "What's wrong with her, sir?" she whispered.

Charlie had gone terribly pale; she feared he might topple from the stool. He clutched the kitchen table's edge with white-knuckled fingers.

"Polly has brown lung," said Dr. Cradock quietly, "and it is nearing its final stages."

Charlie trembled. Mabel struggled to control her thoughts, but the two words played through her mind over and over: *Brown lung, brown lung, brown lung.* It sounded so terrible, like there was something dirty and rotten inside Polly's chest.

"What is that?" Mabel whispered.

"Sadly, it's a common disease among cotton mill workers," said Dr. Cradock. "The jute and cotton dust causes terrible irritation in the lungs. You may have noticed that Miss Wilson wheezes and has trouble breathing sometimes."

Memories struck Mabel like shards of glass. She struggled to hold back her tears as Charlie clasped a hand over his mouth.

"I have," she whispered. "Oh, no! I have. She... she would say she needed to sit down and catch her breath for a minute." Tears filled her eyes. "I should have done something. Why didn't we call you out then?"

"Now, then, Mrs. Finch, you had no way of knowing," said Dr. Cradock. "These cotton mill girls are some of the most stoic people you'll ever meet. Maybe even Polly didn't know that something was wrong."

"What if we keep her out of the dust?" Mabel asked. "She doesn't need to work there. We'll keep her home. We'll manage."

Dr. Cradock hesitated. "Polly certainly can never go back to the cotton mill."

Charlie straightened. "She'll be all right, then. We'll keep her home and she'll be fine."

Dr. Cradock sighed. "I'm terribly sorry, Charlie, but I fear that's not the case. The disease is too advanced."

Charlie stared at the doctor; Mabel guessed the big words made as little sense to him as they did to her.

The doctor sat down across from Charlie and laid one hand on the young blacksmith's brawny arm. The other he laid on Mabel's hand.

"I'm sorry," he said softly. "There's nothing I can do for Polly except to make her comfortable. She's dying."

Charlie snatched his arm away. "No!" he bellowed. "No, she can't be!"

"Mr. Wilson—" Dr. Cradock began.

"Not my Polly." Charlie lurched to his feet, breathing hard, like a fevered bull. "My Polly isn't dying. She's going to be all right. She has to be!"

He crashed out of the cottage.

"Charlie!" Mabel cried, desperate not to be left alone.

His footsteps thundered across the yard. Mabel went to rise, but Dr. Cradock's hand tightened on hers.

"Let him go," he said gently. "We all have different ways of dealing with these things. But I'm afraid you must take my words seriously, Mrs. Finch. I know this must be terrible for you, but it is certain. Polly's lungs are too congested to recover. The brown lung has caused a grievous infection. Her life is measured in days or hours now." He squeezed her hand. "I am so terribly sorry."

"We can get money," said Mabel desperately. "We can sell things and find other doctors, or send her to the hospital. Whatever she needs."

"I'm afraid even the best doctors in the world don't have what she needs," said Dr. Cradock sadly. "She needs a miracle now, Mabel. You can pray and you can give her laudanum; it will still the fevers and soothe her pain. She will die without agony, at least. But that is the best that my human effort can do for her."

He rose then, his face pale and drawn, and gathered up his black bag and hat. Mabel somehow found the strength to walk him to the door and bid him goodbye. There was still no sign of Charlie, but Polly lay alone in the bedroom, so that was where Mabel went.

It seemed difficult to believe she was dying at that moment. Her pinched cheeks and blue lips were softened by the candlelight, and she slept with utter peace, her face drugged into smoothness.

Mabel pulled up a chair and sat beside the bed. She reached for Polly's cold, limp hand and wrapped her fingers around it. It had been a long time since she felt bold and desperate enough to truly pray, but she did it now.

Lord, if You love anyone, it has to be Polly. Save her. Save her!

*****

Charlie came back hours later. Mabel sat by Polly's bedside; she'd barely stirred in all that time, sleeping a drug-laden sleep. But even in her sleep, she coughed at times, and the deadly rattle was always present in her lungs.

Mabel heard his footsteps on the cottage floor, and her quaking heart found a tiny scrap of hope and clung to it. At least, finally, she was no longer alone with Polly—and poor Jack. The little boy had been playing in the other bedroom all this time, quietly keeping himself occupied. He was never this well-behaved. Perhaps he'd seen the terror in his mother's eyes when she told him that Polly was ill and he had to play quietly in Charlie's room for a while.

"Charlie?" Jack's little voice called.

"In a minute, Jack-Jack," Charlie rumbled.

His deep, soft voice made tears of relief sting Mabel's eyes. She wiped them away quickly as Charlie's footsteps approached the bedroom.

"Come in," she called softly.

Charlie opened the door and stood there, staring at Polly. Any anger Mabel might have held toward him dissolved instantly at the sight.

Tears had washed clean trails over his pale cheeks. His big, callused hands shook by his sides, and he took small, gulping breaths as he stared at his sister.

"How... how is she?" he whispered.

"She's sleeping," said Mabel. "Dr. Cradock gave her medicine to help her sleep and take away the pain and fever."

"Will it make her better?" Charlie demanded.

Mabel stared at Polly, longing not to speak the appalling truth. "Maybe," she managed, her voice faltering.

Charlie stumbled into the room. His knees gave way as though weak, and he fell beside the bed, wrapping one hand around Polly's foot. She sighed, but didn't wake.

"Oh, Mae," he whimpered. "Oh, Mae, what will I do without her? She can't die. She—she can't. She's always been there for me. I don't know how to live without her."

The words both frightened and stung Mabel, but she forced her feelings down.

"I don't know," she whispered. "But please don't talk so, not while we're here with her. We don't want to upset her when she wakes."

"If she wakes." Charlie's face crumpled and fresh tears spilled over his cheeks. "I can't bear the thought of living without her, Mabel. How can I survive such a thing? I couldn't. I just couldn't." He buried his face in the sheets and wept. "She always knows what to do. She always makes everything better!"

Tears knotted in Mabel's throat, because it was true. She felt the same way about Polly.

"We have to do something," Charlie moaned. "We have to save her!"

"I'm giving her the medicine," said Mabel, "and when she wakes up I'll give her warm milk and gruel, and—"

"Please, Mae." Charlie released Polly and seized Mabel's arm. "Please. You have to save her."

The weight of his words crashed onto her shoulders as though he had harnessed her to a house. Mabel stared at him.

"Tell me you'll save her." Charlie squeezed her arm, his desperate, fear-crazed eyes boring into hers. "Please, Mabel. Please."

A hundred sensible things flitted through Mabel's mind. *I can't promise that, Charlie. I'll do my best.* But they all seemed pathetic in the face of his fevered terror.

"I won't let her die," Mabel whispered. "I promise."

Comfort flooded into Charlie's expression. The fear remained in the pinched corners of his mouth, but there was peace in his face again.

"Will you give Jack-Jack something to eat, please?" Mabel added, voice cracking.

"Yes. Yes, all right." Charlie straightened. "Call me if—if anything happens."

He stumbled out of the room, and Mabel exhaled. His absence felt like a relief.

*****

The next days followed in a blur. Polly woke only for brief times between doses of medicine, long enough to cough and splutter, sip some gruel, and murmur a few words before she drifted back into her laudanum-induced sleep. Charlie worked, brought home bits of food, and went for the doctor as often as he was able.

It wasn't long before the money ran out with both Mabel and Polly unable to work. It was then that Mabel began to sell the few small treasures she'd gathered over the past for years: an extra pair of shoes, a single good handkerchief, their teapot. Each sale brought a few pennies for Charlie to take to Dr. Cradock and another visit. Each time, he topped up the laudanum bottle and told them again and again that there was nothing he could do.

Wind whipped around the cottage, moaning dismally in its eaves, on the night that the doctor's eyes turned deeply serious as he pressed the cone against Polly's chest. He straightened up slowly and met Mabel's eyes. Between them, Polly slept. Her breaths seemed hard work now, shoulders and hips heaving with each one, and her lips were dry and chapped from breathing through her mouth.

"It won't be long now, Mabel." The past few days had dispensed with formalities. Dr. Cradock laid a kindly old hand on her shoulder. "I'm terribly sorry."

"Is she in pain?" Mabel whispered.

"Not as much as she would be without the laudanum," said Dr. Cradock. "Charlie should say his goodbyes."

Mabel's promise burned like a hot coal on her heart. "He can't."

"Yes." Dr. Cradock looked toward the kitchen and sighed. "I will try one more time to make him see sense."

"There could still be a miracle," said Mabel. "Couldn't there?"

Dr. Cradock looked at her for a long few moments.

"I have long learned that God can do anything, Mabel," he said softly. "If He wills it, He can save her in the blink of an eye. But when He does not heal, we cannot imagine that it is because He cannot heal—or, perhaps worse, because He does not care to heal. We must understand that He allows these things because of a greater plan we cannot see. I, for one, take comfort knowing that Polly knows Him better than anyone I've ever met." He paused. "You and I have both been praying for her miracle, Mabel, and yet perhaps there is no greater miracle than the arrival of a weary soul in the arms of the One to whom it belongs."

Mabel gulped against her tears. "If it's true for anyone, it's true for Polly."

"It's true for all of us." Dr. Cradock squeezed her shoulder. "My prayers are with you, Mabel. If there was more I could do, I would have loved to do it."

He turned and left, his feet quiet on the floorboards. Charlie did not come in; he was putting Jack to bed.

The arms of the One to whom it belongs. Mabel thought of Polly running into the arms of the God she adored so much, and tears filled her eyes. Her heart trusted in it.

But her mind could think of only one thing: what Charlie would do if she failed in her promise.

She glanced at the things waiting on the nightstand for Polly to awake, the cup of milk, the bowl of gruel, the bottle of medicine. Then she wrapped her hands around Polly's and lowered her exhausted head to the covers. She prayed until sleep came for her.

*****

Polly stirred, and Mabel woke instantly.

The candle on the nightstand had burned very low. Polly had slept far longer than usual. Terror gripped Mabel's heart, and her hands tightened over Polly's, whose fingers twitched in response.

"It's... all right... Mabel." Polly squeezed the words out between struggling, rattling breaths.

Mabel raised her head. In the candle's low, guttering light, Polly's face was skeletal. She lay on her back, propped on pillows, her bony chest heaving with the effort of drawing air into her lungs.

Tears stung Mabel's eyes, and she blinked them back quickly.

"Polly," she whispered. *How can you be the one comforting me at a time like this?* she wondered. "Are you hungry?"

"I wouldn't... say no... to milk," Polly croaked.

Mabel warmed the cup over the candle as well as she could. Polly made no effort to take the cup; her limp hands trembled on the covers beside her as Mabel held the cup to her lips.

She took two sips and then coughed, painfully, the sound heavy and damp.

"Here. You're overdue for your medicine," said Mabel. She fumbled for the spoon and bottle. Polly watched in patient silence as Mabel poured medicine into the spoon, then held it to Polly's lips. Swallowing sounded desperately painful.

The simple action left Polly exhausted. She sagged against her pillows, eyes closed, and Mabel thought she would fall asleep again. She wrapped her hands around Polly's once more.

"Mae." Polly swallowed and coughed. "Where… where's Charlie?"

"He's asleep, I think. I'll go and fetch him." Mabel released her hand.

"No." With surprising strength, Polly grasped Mabel's fingers. "It'll do him… no good… to see me… like this."

Mabel sagged into her chair. "What do you need?" she whispered. "What can I do for you?"

Polly's lips twitched. "Everything that… I ever needed… was done for me… on the cross," she whispered. "Don't worry… about me… Mae."

Mabel choked on tears. "Please… don't say that, Polly."

"You know… it's true." Polly gulped air for a few moments, rasping and rattling in her lungs. "I'm not… afraid, you know. I'm going… home to… my Saviour's arms. Don't worry… about me. But if… if he lets you…" Polly paused to cough.

"Don't try to talk," said Mabel. "It's all right. You… you should rest." Her voice cracked.

"I will... peacefully." Polly's lips twitched again, and something gleamed in her eyes, something far beyond the unnatural brightness of laudanum. This was bold and clear and beautiful, an anticipation that went far beyond what Mabel could imagine. "But please... Mae..."

"Anything," said Mabel.

"If Charlie... lets you..." Polly wheezed. "Look after him. If... if he lets you."

Mabel swallowed. She longed to ask Polly what she meant by "if he lets you," but then the girl's hand slackened in hers, and her eyes fluttered closed.

"Polly?" Mabel whispered.

Polly didn't respond. Her breaths were slow and shallow, her eyes sunken and unmoving.

"Oh, Polly." Mabel leaned close and nestled against Polly's cheek. Medicine and illness marred her floral scent. "Oh, Polly, I love you."

She had no idea if Polly ever heard the words. All she knew was that her breaths grew shallower and turned to ragged, irregular gasps. And then she was absolutely still.

Chapter Ten

Mabel sat over Polly's body for what might have been minutes or hours. Polly was as composed in death as she had been in life. Her eyes were closed, her face relaxed, yet it was strangely evident that she was no longer living. Her figure took on a waxiness.

It was a strange experience. It did not feel like being in the room with one who had changed from life to death. It felt like being in the room without someone. Polly had not become a dead thing, Mabel understood with strange clarity. She had gone somewhere else.

She had gone Home, as she always believed she would.

Mabel wanted to weep. She wanted to throw herself on the floor, screaming, but she had to think of Charlie.

Look after him if he lets you, Polly had said. It was the least Mabel could do for the girl whom she'd loved like a sister.

She rose to her feet although her joints felt tight and mechanical, like she'd been made of rusty metal. Her stumbling feet carried her to the door.

She'd thought Charlie was asleep in bed; instead, she found him sitting in his chair by the fire, staring at the dying coals.

"Charlie?" she whispered.

He raised his head, his shoulders tensing. "Is she awake?"

"No." Mabel stared at him. Her words had dried up and blown away like dead leaves in the face of the cold wind of his eyes.

"What, then?" Charlie whispered.

Mabel struggled to find the words, but the despair in his eyes stopped her. She opened her mouth, and only a low moan came out. Her knees turned to water. She sagged to the ground.

"No," Charlie growled. "*No*!"

He pushed past her, almost knocking her over as he ran to the bedroom. Mabel stumbled to her feet and somehow followed. But when she reached the doorway, a terrible, keening shriek ripped through the house, a sound so filled with grief and agony that it was barely human.

"*Noooooooooooo*!" Charlie screamed. "*Polly*!"

"I'm so sorry." The words heaved from Mabel's mouth like vomit. "Charlie, I'm so sorry. I'm so sorry."

Charlie crouched on the bed, Polly's limp body in his arms. Her limbs flopped uselessly as he rocked her, sobbing into her neck.

"Please wake up," he begged her. "Please, Polly, please."

"Mama?" Jack's little voice came from the other bedroom.

"Stay there, Jack-Jack," Mabel quavered.

"Mama, what's happening?" Jack cried.

"Jack, stay there!" Mabel barked.

She hated the horror in his face as he froze in the doorway, but she couldn't let him see the appalling scene playing out before her. Charlie screamed and sobbed. His hands left pale indentations in the body's skin where he clasped the hands and face.

"Charlie..." Mabel whispered.

"Polly," Charlie moaned. "Polly, no. No. No!"

Mabel's heart shattered for him. She stepped nearer and laid a hand on his shoulder, and he whipped around. Despair turned to wild fury in his face.

"*You*," he hissed.

Tears gushed down Mabel's cheeks for the first time. "I'm so sorry, Charlie."

"You promised!" Charlie screamed, a raw roar of fury that knocked her back several steps. "You said you wouldn't let this happen! You wouldn't let her die!"

"I tried," Mabel sobbed. "It wasn't in my power, Charlie. I tried."

"You let her die!" Charlie screamed. "You did this!"

The accusations sank into her like a predator's claws. Mabel's head spun with agony; she wanted to collapse, to allow the floor to swallow her.

"I'm sorry, Charlie," she moaned. "Please—"

"*Get out!*" Charlie shrieked.

Mabel blinked. "Wh-what?"

"Get out of here!" Charlie screamed. "You did this! *You did this*!"

The wildness in his eyes terrified her. She stumbled a few steps back.

"*Go*!" Charlie roared.

"Mama?" Jack cried. "Mama, I'm scared!"

Heartache, terror, and agony tore through Mabel like a wildfire. Her heart pounded in her mouth and her stomach heaved. As the world spun around her, her body became an automaton, enslaved to its basest instinct: to care for her child.

She staggered to Jack, who was crying and extending his pudgy hands to her, and scooped him into her arms. Perhaps if they lay low in this room for the rest of the night, then—

"*GO*!" Charlie bellowed.

She knew it was over then. There was nothing to pack; she had sold everything, and Jack, it seemed, had been put to bed in his clothes. She scooped the child into her arms. He wrapped his arms around her neck and buried his tear-streaked little face in her cheek.

"Mama," he whimpered.

"It's all right, pet. It's all right," Mabel jabbered. "You're all right."

Charlie's screams were wordless now. The agony in them cut into Mabel, but spurred her on. Somehow, in the wild swirl of her grief-stricken thoughts, she understood that she had done this. She'd given him false hope with her foolish promise.

Now she was reaping the reward of her mistake.

She stumbled to the door and shoved it open. Never had this stretch of street and this cobbled yard seemed so cold and alien before. Her heart fluttered in her chest, and Jack shrank away from the frigid spring wind, cowering against her. Her resolve faltered. What about Jack?

"Charlie—" she began.

Something sailed through the open bedroom door and shattered on the doorpost only inches from Mabel's head. Ink and glass sprayed everywhere. It was Polly's inkwell, the one she'd treasured and used so sparingly.

"Get out!" Charlie screamed.

Tears burned Mabel's eyes. She took a deep breath to steady herself, cupped a hand behind her little boy's head, and hurried into the cold.

*****

That was how quickly Mabel and Jack ended up in the same alley where she had almost given birth to him.

It was still the most sheltered place she could find in this area, even all these years later. The wind screamed dismally down the street and poked cold fingers down the alley, but could not quite reach the place where Mabel nestled down behind a pile of broken old boxes that she dragged into a makeshift wall with one hand, the other holding Jack close to her body.

She had no blanket this time. She sat down on the cold stone floor, and felt numb in moments as she hugged Jack against her body. His warmth was the only comfortable thing in her world. Guilt stabbed through her as she realized that, despite it all, Jack had fallen asleep in her arms. She wondered how poorly he'd slept since Polly had fallen ill. How much he'd heard. How much he'd missed having Mabel's arms around him.

"Sleep, my pet," she whispered, kissing his forehead. "Sleep, darling."

She leaned her head against the barrels and tried to find sleep herself, but despite the bone-deep exhaustion sucking at her soul, Mabel couldn't close her eyes. Every time she did, she saw Polly's hollow eyes and heard Charlie's screaming.

Maybe he would come to his senses and find them in the morning. It was the only fragment of hope Mabel had, and she clung to it with all her heart. Yet worry and fear still panged through her limbs, keeping her awake.

She slept in vague, fitful snatches, never too deep, and woke instantly, oriented, when she heard footsteps at the end of the alley. She kept her eyes half shut, trying to be inconspicuous, and through the film of her lashes watched two people edge nearer.

Their manner instantly made worry prickle through her bones. She tried not to hug Jack any tighter. He took small, shallow breaths, his little head pillowed on her chest.

Go away, Mabel willed the men. *Just go away and leave us alone.*

"Oi." One, a man, elbowed the other. "Look."

His companion was a woman in a grubby, dingy dress. "What do you mean, look?"

"Her dress. It ain't half bad," said the man. "Better'n yours. Bout the same size, too."

"Too hard. We'll wake the boy," said the woman.

"That's the best part." The man chuckled. "I heard sweeps and houses are paying two or three shillings for little sweeps or maids."

"Two or three *shillings*?" The woman gasped.

Mabel lay very still, hoping that they would realize the folly of their thoughts and move on.

"That's a lot of money," said the woman wistfully.

"She doesn't look like she'll put up a fight." The man stepped nearer. "I'll grab the boy, you take the dress. Hit her if she fights you."

The woman bunched her hands into fists. "Alright."

They weren't going to back down. The realization shot through Mabel like lightning, and in an instant she was on her feet, Jack crying out in shock as she clutched him.

The woman jumped back. "How now!"

"Grab her!" the man yelled.

He lunged toward Jack, and Mabel whirled away. The woman's fingers closed on her sleeve, her hungry eyes inches from Mabel's, and a terrible, bestial snarl tore from her lips.

"No!" Mabel cried. She reflexively kicked out and her shoe connected with the woman's shin.

The woman howled.

"Come here, you wretched thing!" The man lunged again.

Mabel whirled around and bolted, hugging Jack to her body. It was like trying to sprint away while heavily pregnant, except that Jack sobbed in her ear now instead of bouncing in her belly, and her fear was a thousand times more real as it rushed through her body with every ragged breath. She flung herself down the alley and bolted down a block of factories before she finally realized that no one had given chase.

Jack was still crying when she stumbled to a halt. Mabel hugged him, shaking, her head swinging left and right as she searched for her enemies. But there was no sign of the two would-be robbers. Instead, she spotted the reason they hadn't chased her: a bobby on the beat. The policeman whistled to himself quietly as he swung his truncheon by its string. A bell hung from his belt, soundless now, and he wore a tall black hat decorated with silver insignias.

Perhaps she could ask him for help. Mabel stepped forward, rocking Jack in an attempt to calm him.

His eyes found Mabel and narrowed. "Get off the street," he barked.

"Yes, sir. Of course, sir," Mabel stammered.

She turned and scampered away as though she had somewhere to go. Instead, she turned into the first gaping black doorway of an abandoned building she saw.

Dust hung in the interior. Mabel's gut lurched as she realized what this factory had once been.

A cotton mill. Like the one that had killed Polly.

She almost tripped over a bale of cotton. Dust puffed into the air, making Jack cough between his cries. Horrified, Mabel backed away from the bale and stumbled into the next room, where sheafs of half-woven fabric lay abandoned. She tried not to wonder what might have happened here, her thoughts wandering painfully toward the idea of the plague or the pox. It was warm and dry, and as the first thrum of raindrops striking the roof sounded, she knew it was her best chance of keeping her child alive.

That was all that mattered now: keeping Jack alive. Maybe it was all that had ever mattered to Mabel.

She sagged down on a roll of rough fabric and hugged him close, rocking him back and forth as she crooned lullabies in his ear. He didn't fall asleep again as she'd hoped. Instead, his sobs quietened into slow breaths, but she could still see the gleam of his open eyes in the sliver of streetlight falling through a broken window.

"Mama?" he whispered.

Mabel stroked his hair. "Yes, Jack-Jack?"

"Can we go home now?" Jack asked.

Mabel didn't think it possible for her heart to shatter further, but somehow it did. "I'm sorry, pet. We're not going home now."

"When?" Jack insisted.

Mabel gave him the only nugget of hope she had, like a mother bird passing the last worm to her young. "When Charlie comes to find us."

"How much longer?" Jack whispered. "I'm scared. It's so cold. Why are people chasing us?"

"I don't know, pet." Mabel wrestled with her tears. "I don't know."

Jack huddled closer to her. He was silent for a few more moments and Mabel had begun to hope he'd fallen asleep when he spoke again.

"Is Polly dead?"

Mabel's arms tightened around him. Where had a four-year-old learned the concepts of life and death? She didn't know how to explain them to him.

"Yes," she managed. "I'm sorry, pet. Polly's gone to heaven. She's died."

Jack gripped her dress in small, chubby fists. "I want her back."

"We won't see her again in our lives, Jack-Jack." Mabel swallowed the lump in her throat. "I'm sorry."

"I want Polly," Jack whispered. "I want Charlie."

Mabel pressed his face to her chest. "I know, pet. So do I." Her voice broke. "So do I."

*****

It was when Jack coughed that Mabel knew it was over.

She had tried. She fought bitterly for three long, rainy days to keep them alive on the brutal streets. She'd started by going back to the factory, falling to her knees before Mr. Compton, and begging for her job back with tears flowing down her cheeks. Mr. Compton kicked mud into her face and told her to get out of his sight.

Since then, Mabel spent every day going from one factory to the next, pleading for work. Sometimes Jack walked; most of the time, she carried the weary, hunger-weakened child. Most of the men at the factories were merely rude. Several cursed, and one threatened to set his dog on her.

At night, they slept in the warehouse. Every evening Mabel tried begging from the crowds, but they were as impoverished as she. None had a penny to spare. Only on one blessed evening did she find a stale bread roll lying on a rubbish heap. She snatched it before anyone else could and gave it to Jack; he wolfed it down in giant bites.

A thousand times a day, she heard, "Mama, I'm hungry." But on the third day, Jack stopped asking.

And Charlie did not come.

Twice, Mabel almost went back to the cottage. It was so nearby, filled with all the comforts of home—a warm bed, a hot fire, the prospect of food. She remembered the way it smelled when Polly made scones, a rare and wonderful treat. But she never did. Polly's ghost hung over that place, and she would never forget Charlie's vengeful eyes.

On the third day, as evening's chill seeped into London's air, Mabel stumbled down a side street. She had ceased feeling hunger; it had been replaced with steady weakness.

Her eyelids felt leaden. Her numb feet dragged on the stones, and Jack weighed a thousand pounds in her arms, his hands linked at the back of her neck. His pale face lay on her shoulder, eyes closed. She hoped he was sleeping.

Mabel's weary eyes found a gentleman striding down the street. Though his coat was patched, its thickness spoke of good make. He carried an ebony cane and the chain of a brass pocket watch peeked from his coat.

"Please, sir." Mabel started toward him, supporting Jack with one hand and holding out the other. "I haven't eaten in days. I—"

"Don't beg, woman." The man stepped aside as though fearful of catching poverty from her breath. "Take yourself to the workhouse if you're hungry. That's where my contributions go."

He stormed away, and that dreaded word slid down Mabel's spine like a shower of ice. *Workhouse*. So many had spoken it to her over the past three days, and yet there was always fear in their eyes when they did.

She turned to keep walking, hoping to try the factories down the block, and that was when Jack raised his head and coughed. It was only once, but it was a terribly familiar sound, deep and phlegmy, and it came from inside his chest.

"Jack?" Mabel stopped. "Are you all right, pet?"

Jack raised his head and stared at her with bright, reddened eyes. Mabel touched his cheeks and winced at the heat.

"So tired, Mama," Jack whispered, then laid his head on her shoulder once more.

Mabel's heart galloped in her chest like the poor old horse with the shattered wagon behind him all those years ago. Jack was sick, just like Polly, and Polly had died: she had had a warm bed and a doctor and medicine, and she had still died.

Jack had none of those things.

Mabel didn't cry. It felt as though her tears had dried up, her soul wrung out.

"It's all right, pet," she whispered. "You're going to be all right. We—we're going to a place where they'll have food and medicine for you."

Jack didn't respond; he'd fallen asleep with his head on her shoulder.

Mabel scraped together her courage, turned around, and set off for the nearest workhouse.

*****

The great building had few chimneys and even fewer windows. Those that were present seemed too small for large rooms and stood in regimented lines, as if too afraid to deviate from one another even a little. The long, squat building had two stories, and its bare brick glared in the sun, but at least there were no holes in the walls.

Mabel clutched Jack tightly, his sleeping body heavy in her tired arms, as she edged up to the fence. It was made of wrought iron with horrid spikes at the top. She wondered if it was meant to keep people out—or in.

The heavy double doors were closed, but the gate stood open enough for Mabel to squeeze herself through. As she approached, she tried not to look at the stone-paved yards visible through the fence on either side of her. Men sat in one, women in another. It made sense that they would separate men and women, she supposed, trying not to look at the bony backs of the men as they tapped rocks with hammers and chisels, breaking them into smaller pieces. The women seemed busy with picking bits of old rope apart. It seemed fruitless, but at least they were alive.

Unlike Polly. Unlike Jack would be, if she didn't do this.

She reached up, her other arm aching with Jack's weight, and knocked on the door. It was only then that she realized none of the women in the yard had babies or children with them, although many were her age.

Mabel's heart plummeted, but it was too late. The door swung open and a stout woman with heavy jowls and downturned lips glared at her.

"Please, ma'am," Mabel whispered. "I have nowhere else to go, and my little boy—"

"Sick as a dog, is he? Small wonder. You vagrants think you can keep children alive. Fools!" The woman shook her head. "Get inside."

"Can you help him?" Mabel shuffled into the hall.

The woman slammed the door behind her, making her jump.

"That's what we're here for, isn't it?" she barked. "This way."

She strode down a bleak, undecorated hallway that smelled vaguely of urine and cheap soap. Mabel's heart hammered as she followed her. They paused outside a regimented office, where another woman sat behind a desk, wearing a hat with a bright yellow flower in it. The flower was the only colour in the whole workhouse, as far as Mabel could tell.

"Two newcomers," the matron barked.

The woman behind the desk opened a large book without looking up. "Names and ages."

The matron glared at Mabel.

She cleared her throat and stuttered the words. "M-Mabel and Jack Finch. He's four... I'm..." She stopped. "Twenty-two or twenty-three. I'm not sure."

The woman at the desk jotted something in her book. "All right, carry on."

"This way," the matron snapped.

Jack slumbered on as Mabel carried him to the next room: a gigantic bathroom. A metal tub stood in one corner with two barrels beside it. A ladle was hooked on the steaming one, but a bucket drifted in the cold water of the other barrel.

"Strip," the matron ordered.

"E-excuse me?" Mabel whispered.

"Get those filthy clothes off. You'll infect the whole workhouse with your lice or scabies or whatever else you have," the matron snapped.

Mabel hovered in the corner, but the matron made no attempt to leave. Instead, she methodically slopped cold water from the barrel into the tub, using the bucket.

"I—" Mabel began.

"Now!" the matron said. "Do you think I have time for your dithering, woman?"

Mabel's hands shook as she gently unbuttoned Jack's clothes and pulled them off. He had grown so thin in the few days they'd been on the streets; the sight of his protruding backbone made her sick to her stomach. He'd get food here, she knew. That thought was the only thing that lent her the strength to peel off her own clothing, keeping Jack balanced on her shoulder as she did. He didn't wake. She knew that it was the fever making his sleep so deep.

She trembled, naked, clutching his tiny body to hers. The matron sneered as she looked Mabel up and down. She added a couple of ladles of hot water to the tub.

"Get in," she ordered.

Mabel stumbled nearer, shame and terror making her heart pound. The matron never looked away as she lowered herself and Jack into the water. When her buttocks touched the cold surface, she yelped with surprise.

"Please, ma'am," she stammered. "He's sick, and it's so cold—"

"Silence," the matron ordered. "You couldn't provide for your child. You're in no position to complain about what others have given you from the kindness of their hearts." Her sneer grew. "Beggars can't be choosers."

"Yes, ma'am." Mabel hung her head.

Jack yelped and woke when she lowered him into the water. "Mama, no," he protested.

"It's all right, Jack-Jack. It's all right," Mabel whispered.

The matron gave her a rough sponge and a penny-sized cake of very hard soap, and Mabel did her best, working the soap into Jack's hair and smoothing it over his body. She did the same for herself; despite the cold, there was something relieving about getting the chunks of dirt out of her hair. Jack was trembling when the matron finally handed her a small, rough towel. Mabel wrapped him in it and rubbed his hair dry, trying to keep his head warm.

"Don't worry about that," the matron snapped. "It's going to be shaved in any case."

Mabel ran her hand through Jack's damp hair. The rich brown of his curls gleamed under the brutal gas light. "Shaved?" she whispered. "He doesn't have lice."

"They all say that," said the matron. "Come on, dry off."

Jack sat in a miserable, coughing heap on the floor, wrapped in his towel, while Mabel hastily worked her towel over her body. The matron finally handed her two sets of clothes: a shirt and pants for Jack and a dress for her, both shapeless and ugly, made from coarse fabric striped in black and white. Mabel was so desperate not to be naked in front of this woman that she would have gladly donned sackcloth. She tucked Jack into his clothes, then pulled the dress over her head, exhaling with relief as it settled around her body.

Another woman stepped into the room without knocking. She was painfully thin, with dull grey eyes.

"Here's the boy." The matron jerked her head toward Jack, who was in Mabel's arms again.

"All right." The grey-eyed woman stepped forward. "Give him to me."

Mabel hesitated, arms tightening around her child. "Where are you taking him?"

"To the children's dorm," said the woman.

Mabel's heart skipped. She remembered the women in the yard, all without babies or children.

"But—but he's mine," she whispered. "You're not taking him away from me, are you?"

"Of course we are," the matron snapped. "Did you think you'd be a happy little family here in the workhouse?"

Mabel stared at her in mute horror. She squeezed Jack so hard that he whimpered in protest.

"You can't provide for your child," the matron hissed. "You relinquish your rights to him as his mother."

"No," Mabel whispered, hugging Jack close.

"Is this going to take long? I've left them in the classroom. I don't want the bullies to cause trouble while I'm gone," said the grey-eyed woman.

"Please." Tears returned to Mabel's eyes. "Please don't take him away from me."

"Hand over the child or return to the streets," the matron barked, "with a fine for wasting my time, soap, and water."

Mabel trembled. The grey-eyed woman stepped closer. With all her heart, she wanted to scream, *No!* and flee from this awful place with her child.

Then Jack gave another cough and raised his head. "You're hurting me, Mama," he whispered.

She knew he meant that she was squeezing him too tight, but he was right in more ways than one. She *was* hurting him. She'd let Polly die, and now they were on the streets, and he was sick.

It was her fault. The matron was right. She couldn't care for her own child.

She kissed his forehead. "I love you, Jack-Jack," she croaked.

Jack blinked at her. "Mama, what's wrong?"

"I'm sorry, baby," Mabel moaned, as she had done so many times when he was yet unborn. "I'm so sorry."

She kissed him again, but the grey-eyed woman's patience was spent. She grabbed Jack roughly under his arms and hoisted him to the ground. "Come on. You can walk."

"Mama, who is she?" Jack cried.

"Go with her, Jack-Jack." Mabel forced her tears back. "It's all right. Everything's all right. Go with the nice lady. I'll see you soon."

Jack stared at her. The woman tugged at his hand, and he stumbled after her, but he didn't look away from Mabel.

His scared, confused eyes stayed on her until she had pulled him out of the room.

Every part of Mabel trembled. She thought she might be sick.

"You're too late for dinner." The matron sneered. "Straight to the dormitory. You'll get gruel at breakfast."

Mabel knew it would be polite to thank her, but she could not squeeze the words through her lips. Head hanging, she followed the matron down the cold hallway. Her hands were empty.

Her tears flowed.

*****

Percy Mitchell's living room fire leaped and roared, filling the space with its warm, golden light. He leaned back in his comfortable, high-backed armchair, his newspaper open on his lap, and peered at the tightly printed text through the glasses he was forced to wear after nearly five years of scouring these papers after dark.

A comfortably proportioned woman padded through from the kitchen, carrying a tray of tea. She set it on the table at his left.

"Oh, Mr. Mitchell," she said. "Don't tell me you're looking through them London papers again."

Percy grimaced apologetically at his elderly housekeeper. "I have to, Mrs. Minnow."

"You've been doing this far too long, dear. It's not natural," said Mrs. Minnow in a motherly tone. "You don't even know if the girl still lives in London, for Pete's sake."

"The train conductor said she took the late train there," said Percy. "It's the only way I can think of to find her."

"It's been so long, dear," said Mrs. Minnow. "Perhaps she's forgotten all about the farm."

"It still legally belongs to her," said Percy. "I knew it the moment I saw that forged will and met the dreadful Davies couple. They barely knew how to write a forgery, let alone sign Ned's name, and they didn't have the good sense to get rid of the original will. I found it in five minutes' search of that house."

"Yes, dear, and the police carted them off. They've gotten what's coming to them," said Mrs. Minnow, "but Mrs. Finch is never coming back. If she wanted the farm, she would have returned."

Percy sighed. "Maybe. But I can't ride past that farm every day and see it lying abandoned and fallow without thinking of her, Mrs. Minnow. What if she's in poverty? London isn't kind to anyone, least of all women. That farm could change her life if only she knew she had it."

"You've done more than enough," said Mrs. Minnow. "Nobody would expect you to keep searching, Mr. Mitchell."

"I suppose." Percy took his teacup. "Thank you, Mrs. Minnow."

"Goodnight, sir," said the housekeeper.

"Goodnight," Percy murmured.

Mrs. Minnow withdrew, and Percy sipped his tea slowly, staring into the flames. He remembered a girl with soft blue eyes and long, thick locks of brunette hair. He remembered the fear in her eyes, but more than that: firm courage, dauntless persistence, and the ability to think and act decisively.

He'd never met anyone like Mabel Finch, and he knew that farm was rightfully hers.

Percy set down his teacup and squinted down at the paper through his glasses. His eye skimmed over the lines as he had done so many evenings for so many years. Sleepiness made his eyelids heavy. He'd skim one more page, he thought, and then it was time for bed.

Then, the words caught his eye.

Mabel Finch.

Percy almost knocked over his teacup in his excitement. He gripped the paper tightly, tilting it to catch the firelight, and read the announcement.

Mr. Charles Wilson of Deptford Creek proudly announces his engagement to Mrs. Mabel Finch.

Percy lunged to his feet. "I've found her!" he cried. "Mrs. Minnow, I've found her!"

The housekeeper blundered into the room. "Mr. Mitchell, are you all right?"

"All right? I'm wonderful!" Percy laughed and grabbed the old woman's arm. "I've found Mabel Finch."

"What! Where?" cried Mrs. Minnow.

"Deptford Creek, London." Percy showed her the paper. "I have to go and find her. I have to tell her about the farm!"

Mrs. Minnow shook her head. "Write her a letter."

"My dear Mrs. Minnow," said Percy, "there's no address. I'm going to London."

He kissed the housekeeper on the cheek, making her giggle like a girl, and bounded from the room. It was only when he was already in his bedroom, packing, that he realized the full extent of the announcement.

Mr. Charles Wilson announces his engagement...

Percy hesitated, staring down at his suitcase, remembering those perfect blue eyes. A swift pang of disappointment ran through him. Then he shook his head, chiding himself for his ridiculousness. There were greater reasons to go to London than simply because he thought Mabel Finch was the bravest and most beautiful woman he'd ever seen.

"Lord, go with me," he prayed quietly, and continued packing.

Part Four

Chapter Eleven

One Year Later

The stone floor was cold on Mabel's hands and knees, but after a year, the calluses had grown so that she barely felt the pain anymore. She worked mechanically, her mind far away as she worked the scrubbing brush over the floor's unyielding surface.

The sound of scrubbing filled the hallway. They were right outside the men's dormitory now, and soon they would enter it and start cleaning there, too—dealing with the disgusting lice and appalling smells that crept from the bedding, or with vomit and urine in the corners when sick men had been unable to rouse themselves to the horrific lavatories before they were taken to the infirmary. Twenty other women worked alongside Mabel, plying their brushes on the floors and walls, some standing on buckets to reach above the window.

The window.

Chores rotated through the workhouse. Mabel hated all of them, especially laundry, when she was forced to wash dozens of little shirts and little trousers that may have been Jack's or not, in a steaming room filled with the caustic stench of soap that left her hands chapped and bleeding. But once every two weeks, Mabel's group had their turn to scrub this particular men's dormitory, and Mabel lived for these days.

She listened intently for the church bells outside. At one o'clock exactly, the little boys finished their turn in the dining hall, and they would walk around the outside of the workhouse to their classroom. That was when they were all visible through the men's dormitory window.

That was when she could see Jack.

Anxiety clawed at the inside of her belly. She forced it down and kept working, scrubbing hard as she edged nearer and nearer to the dormitory door. If she missed a spot, the matron would scream at her, but she didn't care. All she wanted was to see Jack.

No punishment could be worse than missing him again.

As she had done thousands of times, she thought about her last time in the men's dormitory two weeks ago. She'd rushed to the window at two o'clock to witness a tide of listless little boys flow down the passage outside, and she had not seen the thick brown curls of her son.

Maybe he was in the infirmary or maybe they had cut his hair again and she'd lost him in the mass of children. Mabel wasn't sure. She knew he had to be alive; the matron had come to tell other women in her group about their children's deaths a few times in the year she had been here.

Some of those women had been separated from their children for years, but Mabel would never forget their keening when they heard the news. One had died of a broken heart shortly after.

Mabel knew she would share that fate if she lost Jack. But he had to be alive. He had to be with the other little boys, and she simply had to see him today.

The church bell chimed a quarter to two. Mabel worked faster. She was in the dormitory now, and she scrubbed in a straight line toward the window, praying that their supervisor would stay in the hall with the bulk of the women.

It nearly worked. When the clock struck two, Mabel was six feet from the window. She lunged to her feet and grabbed the windowsill, almost striking her head on the grimy glass as she strove to see into the passage.

"Hey!" her supervisor shouted. "You're meant to be working, you lazy wretch!"

Mabel ignored her. She strained her eyes as the teacher strode past, back straight, hair tied back sharply, and the group of little boys trudged lifelessly after her.

Mabel searched, heart pounding, hands against the window. Where was Jack? Where was her precious son?

"I'm talking to you!" her supervisor shouted.

Mabel didn't care. Her heart raced faster as she looked through all the boys again, but she saw none of them with dark brown hair. It was hard to see their faces from this distance, but she was certain she didn't see Jack.

"Finch!" her supervisor barked, grabbing her shoulder.

Mabel whipped around. Anger she'd pent up for a full year burst from her in a roar that echoed around the dormitory. "*Where is my son?*"

The supervisor, a woman about Mabel's age, stumbled back. Her eyes filled with fear for a moment, then narrowed.

"You have no son, workhouse wretch," she barked. "You gave him up. Get back to work." She pointed imperiously at Mabel's bucket and brush.

Mabel didn't care. Her veins felt as though they had been filled with fire. She grabbed the front of the woman's dress, making her squeal. "I asked you a question. Where is Jack? Where is my boy?"

"What is going on here?" the matron shouted.

Mabel's heart froze. She released the supervisor, who scrambled back with a terrified cry.

Mrs. Jones, the cruel matron Mabel had met on her first night here, stormed into the dormitory. Her eyes flashed fire as she faced Mabel. She leaned on a slender bamboo cane.

"You, Finch," she growled. "What are you doing? Get back to work."

The other women cowered against the walls, wide-eyed, clutching their brushes like shields.

"She accosted me, Mrs. Jones!" the supervisor cried. "She seized me!"

"I want to know where my son is," Mabel growled. She raised her chin, meeting Mrs. Jones' eyes. "Where is Jack Finch?"

Mrs. Jones' eyes narrowed. "I told you on your first day, Finch, that you have relinquished all rights to the child you brought into the world but failed to provide for." She raised her cane and slapped it into her opposite palm with an appalling sound—wood upon flesh. "You have no right to enquire about him. You will return to work at once or face punishment."

Mabel's terror and fury made her reckless. She took a step toward Mrs. Jones, her hands clenched into fists. "Tell me where my boy is. Tell me if he's safe." Her voice cracked on the last syllable.

Mrs. Jones raised her cane, and Mabel's courage left her. She cried out and raised her hands over her head.

"I thought so," Mrs. Jones sneered. "You insolent wench. You will be told nothing. How dare you lay your hands on an employee of the workhouse? I should cast you out!"

Mabel's knees turned to water. She almost fell, cowering, before the matron.

"Please. Please don't do that," she whimpered. "Please. This is the only place where I can be close to him. I won't do it again."

"Very well," said Mrs. Jones. "Left hand."

Tears stung Mabel's eyes, but she wept for the boy she hadn't seen, not for what was about to happen to her. She held out her left hand—the one that she didn't need as much for work—and braced herself.

Mrs. Jones raised the cane, and it landed hard across the palm of Mabel's hand. The blow brought pain, then tingling numbness. The second blow reawakened the pain, and it grew worse with the third and fourth and fifth, creeping from her hand down to her wrist and forearm. She gritted her teeth against it, waiting for it to be over. It was nothing compared to the agony in her chest; her heart felt as though it had been ripped from between her ribs.

"There," said Mrs. Jones. "Now you'll think twice about threatening your superiors, won't you, Finch?"

"Yes, Mrs. Jones," Mabel whispered.

"Get back to work," Mrs. Jones barked. "No more slacking off. And you, girl, keep these women in line."

The supervisor cringed as though afraid she would be next to be caned. "Yes, Mrs. Jones." She turned to Mabel, eyes flashing, and kicked the scrubbing brush toward her. It collided with Mabel's knees, splashing water on her skirt. "You heard her. Scrub!"

Mabel ducked her head. Tears spilled down her cheeks as she gripped the brush in both hands, ignoring the pain from her left, and worked it back and forth across the stone floor. Each motion of the brush drove the question in her heart in deeper, like a dagger plunged into her flesh.

Where is Jack? Where is Jack? Where is Jack?

*****

They worked all day. When the bell rang for supper, the supervisor told Mabel with a sneer that she was to stay behind and scrub out the last corners of the hallway. Mabel knew they had already been scrubbed. She knew she was being punished.

She knew that her swollen hand would only be all the more sore tomorrow.

And none of this was worse than knowing that her only hope, her only anchor to the memory of joy, had been torn away from her.

She scrubbed, shoulders aching, hand stinging fiercely, a smear of blood on the brush from a burst blister. All this time, she had kept going in the workhouse because she believed Jack was here. Walls and hallways separated her from him, but at least they were in the same building. At least she knew where her little boy was.

Now, that hope had been plucked away from her like the ground from beneath her feet. She was tumbling into an abyss of despair.

"Oh, Lord!" she cried, her shaking arms struggling to work the brush into the corners. "Lord my God, why would You do this to me? Where is my child? How can I go on?"

Her cries echoed around the empty hallway. Mabel hardly cared who heard her, as long as the only Friend she had left was listening. At least, she hoped He was still a friend to her. It felt as though He'd left her a year ago, the night Polly had died, taking every good thing in Mabel's life with her.

Her arms would work the brush no longer. Numb and exhausted, they fell into her lap.

"Please," she sobbed aloud. "God, please. I know I haven't prayed much or been attentive in church often. It's hard not to fall asleep in the chapel on Sundays. I don't know if You're listening, but You're all I have left. Oh, Lord, all I know is that I need You. Father, help me!"

Her desperate cry rang through the rafters and ended in a sob. She hung her head, gritting her teeth against the weeping that threatened to crush her. The agony in her heart was so much worse than the pangs running through her hand where it rested in her lap.

"Help me," she whispered.

The miracle that follows was not heralded by angels with trumpets, nor did she see any chariots of fire. All that happened was that Mabel's pounding heart slowed. Something strange settled over her heart, wrapping her as though in a warm fleece blanket.

She opened her eyes slowly, startled by the stillness within her. No, not quite stillness—it ran deeper than that.

Peace, Mabel realized. For the first time, she felt a peace that surpassed her understanding. It covered over her worry and fear, even eased her pain.

Everything is going to be all right, Mabel realized. She didn't know how; she didn't know where Jack was or if she would ever see him again, yet she knew that all would be well. The strange certainty anchored itself deep in her soul—or perhaps her soul anchored itself to the certainty. Either way, Mabel felt like someone who had been falling a long time, and at last landed safely in a warm, springy embrace.

She closed her eyes and exhaled, and when the matron's voice ripped down the hallway, it hardly made her jump at all.

"*Finch!*" Mrs. Jones barked. "Mabel Finch!"

Mabel rose, holding her brush. "Yes, Mrs. Jones," she said calmly.

The matron appeared around the bend in the hallway, scowling.

"There you are," she snapped.

Mabel hardly knew what would come next. Another caning? A night in the refractory ward? Whatever came next, she would face it with this new, strange peace. "Yes, Mrs. Jones," she said again.

Mrs. Jones sneered. "Come with me at once."

Mabel hung her head. "Yes, Mrs. Jones."

She replaced her brush in her bucket and carried it with her, holding her injured hand curled close to her chest, as she followed Mrs. Jones down the hallway. The matron headed for her office—that dreaded place near the front of the workhouse where inmates only ever visited for three purposes: to arrive, to leave, or to be sentenced to some severe punishment. Half rations for a week? Mabel didn't know what awaited her. She trembled, but she was ready to face it.

The matron pushed the door open. "I'm sorry to keep you waiting, Mr. Mitchell."

It had been over five years since Mabel had heard that name, but it was like a glorious note of music cutting through the cacophony of her life. Instantly, the image of a kind face filled her mind. A gentle smile. Warm brown eyes and wings of dark hair. Something fluttered deep within her.

Percy Mitchell. The lawyer who had been so good to her near Ned's death.

She shook herself, dislodging the image. No, she was being foolish. She'd misheard. Or the matron was speaking to some other Mr. Mitchell. It was a common enough name.

Then he spoke. "It's no trouble at all. Thank you for your time."

The warmth, the kindness—and the wonderful, sweet depth of the accent, so different from London's harsh vowels. It was a country accent, one which Mabel hadn't heard in nearly six years.

"Here she is," said Mrs. Jones. "Step inside, Mrs. Finch."

Mabel barely registered the matron's change in tone. Somehow her feet carried her into the office, and Percy Mitchell stood by the desk. Five years had hardly changed him. The creases around his eyes were deeper, but they were still just as kind. His jet-black hair still gleamed where it fell over his forehead.

His smile still cut right into her heart.

"Mabel," he gasped, his smile faltering. His eyes widened as he stared at her, perhaps seeing the changes poverty had etched in her.

"Percy?" she croaked. "Percy Mitchell? Is that really you?"

Tears flooded Percy's eyes, making them larger and brighter. He quickly blinked them back.

"I can't believe I finally found you," he said.

"What are you doing here?" Mabel managed.

Percy's smile returned, and he held out his hands. He made no effort to touch her, but waited until she slowly placed her good hand in his. She kept the wounded one by her chest.

"I'm here to take you away from this terrible place," he said.

"I beg your pardon!" Mrs. Jones cried.

Percy raised his head, dark eyes flashing with a strength Mabel hadn't seen there before. "Gather Mrs. Finch's things at one, ma'am. I am leaving with her."

"No. Wait," Mabel cried, her hand tightening on Percy's. "I'm sorry. I—I can't go. I have to be with Jack."

"Jack?" Percy asked.

"My child." Mabel looked into his face. "Ned's son. I... I was expecting him when Ned died. We've been separated in this place for a year. I'm so sorry. I can't leave Jack."

She tried to tug her hand away from his, but Percy's grip tightened on her fingers, gentle but immovable.

"No mother is expected to leave her little one," he said quietly. "Mrs. Jones, if you please, I request that you bring the boy out to his mother at once."

Mrs. Jones' scowl deepened. "I'm afraid that's not possible."

Mabel sucked in a terrified breath. The peace in her held, but she couldn't speak.

"Why not?" Percy raised his chin. "What happened to the boy?"

"Nothing happened to him, Mr. Mitchell, and I don't appreciate your tone," said Mrs. Jones. "Young Mr. Finch was…" She paused. "He was hired out."

Percy's hands clenched into fists. "I've read about what you workhouses do with children. You sold him, didn't you?"

"We are not in the practice of slavery," said Mrs. Jones. "Mr. Finch became a pauper apprentice to a chimney-sweep."

"A chimney-sweep!" Mr. Mitchell roared. "Don't you know that the chimneys are poisonous to little children?"

Mabel's head spun. Jack. Her sweet, poor little Jack-Jack, sweeping chimneys. She imagined him squeezing his tiny body into those tight, claustrophobic spaces, filled with soot. She imagined how afraid he was.

"At least young Mr. Finch has a future now," said Mrs. Jones harshly.

"Why, woman, I should—" Percy stopped. "Mabel, are you all right?"

Mabel could make no sound. The last thing she saw before the room faded to darkness was the worry in Percy's eyes as he lunged to catch her.

Chapter Twelve

Mabel woke to clean sheets.

The feeling was so alien to her that for a few moments she thought she was dreaming. Surely it was impossible that she was truly lying in a bed alone, a real bed, not a pallet she had to share with at least one other woman. She hadn't slept in anything like this since the farm.

The farm. Percy. Jack!

Mabel's eyes snapped open. She lay in a comfortable, wallpapered room, with sunlight shining through the window and clean, warm blankets draped over her. A girl of thirteen or fourteen sat in a stool beside her, quietly reading.

Mabel sat up, and the girl raised her head.

"Ah, Mrs. Finch," she said. "You're awake."

"Where am I?" Mabel asked. "Where's Jack?"

"I don't know any Jack, ma'am, but you're in an inn at the edge of Deptford Creek," said the girl. "Mr. Mitchell had you brought here after you fainted. Are you feeling better?"

Mabel nodded dumbly; her spinning head had steadied, and she realized that someone had bound up her injured hand.

"We gave you a little wash. I hope you don't mind, but the housekeeper and me thought you must be so uncomfortable," said the girl. "Here—I burned those horrid workhouse things after Mr. Mitchell carried you here."

"He… carried me here?" Mabel managed.

"Of course he did. He's quite in love with you," said the girl.

Mabel didn't know what to make of those words. Percy had certainly never acted inappropriately toward her, yet the sparkle in his eyes… A jolt of excitement ran through her, and she hastily crushed it.

"Here," said the girl. She rose and went to the wardrobe, then took out a sturdy blue dress. "The housekeeper ran to a shop for you. I think it'll fit all right. If you're hungry, go ahead and put it on, and you can join Mr. Mitchell downstairs for breakfast."

Mabel still felt lost in a dream when she drifted downstairs a few minutes later, her hair brushed, the new dress warm and sturdy on her body. The dining hall was small and quiet, but nothing was out of place. The guests wore warm clothes and ate from porcelain plates, not tin. The girl from upstairs helped a few other servers to bring dishes to the guests.

Her eyes found Percy instantly. He sat at the back of the room alone, sipping tea and gazing out of the window.

"Mr. Mitchell," said Mabel quietly.

Percy looked up. His eyes widened briefly as they rested on her, but he didn't stare too long. "Please call me Percy," he said. "Have a seat. You must be starving."

Mabel thought she was too confused to be hungry until a servant came by with two plates of scones, each with butter and cheese and thick red strawberry jam. She hadn't eaten like this in so many years that she barely remembered how to cut the scone. She couldn't wait to add the jam and cheese; she thrust the buttered scone into her mouth and bit down, then almost cried when the wonderful, fluffy, buttery flavours filled her mouth.

Guilt followed sharply. She set down the scone, wiped her mouth and said, "Do you know where Jack is?"

"Not yet," said Percy. "When you fainted, I rushed back here with you. I feared you were very ill." His cheeks coloured. "I'm sorry; I should have stayed to find out about Jack, but I'll go back to the workhouse and enquire after breakfast."

"You will?" said Mabel.

"Of course. You should stay here and rest," said Percy gently.

His kindness made tears sting her eyes, but she held them back. "What are you doing here, Percy?"

He told her everything as she ate her scones. By the time he'd ordered her a second helping, Mabel knew the whole story: how he'd known that the will was fake as soon as Alf and Ada brought it to him, how he'd found Ned's real will and that it left the farm to Mabel, and how he'd had Alf and Ada arrested. Then he had searched endlessly for Mabel for nearly five years before he saw her name in the paper with Charlie's engagement announcement. It had taken him another year to track her down at the workhouse.

Mabel didn't stop eating although her jaw wanted to drop. "Ned... Ned left the farm to me?" she whispered.

Percy nodded. "It's yours, Mabel, all of it. The house, the barn—everything."

Mabel sagged in her chair. "Six years," she said. "Nearly six years you've been searching for me."

Percy looked away. "It was only right. I should have offered to help you with Ned's will. I could have prevented all of your suffering."

Mabel sipped her tea. "Have you found out anything about Charlie?"

"No," said Percy. "I'm afraid not. I came straight to the workhouse after I found your name in the paper, you see." He flushed. "I'll enquire, if you like."

"No," said Mabel. She looked away. "No... no, Charlie made it quite clear that... that he wasn't interested in me."

She finished her tea slowly, then set it down, marvelling at the feeling of a full stomach. With it came worry. This was all so wonderful that it couldn't possibly be real.

"Thank you very much for the breakfast, Percy," she said carefully. "I can go to the workhouse and ask about my son. I'll pay the inn back for the dress, too, as soon as I can."

Percy stared up at her, confused. "Mabel, please, don't look so worried. I've already paid for the dress. You don't owe anyone anything."

Mabel hesitated.

"I'm in London on business," Percy gently explained. "I'll be here another week. In the meantime, we'll search for Jack, and you can travel back to the country with me when I return. Then you can take ownership of your farm." He paused, doubt flickering in his eyes. "If you would like that."

The farm. Mabel had dreamed of showing it to Jack so many times. She had to struggle to hold back her tears.

"I would love that," she admitted softly.

Percy's smile broke over his face like sunrise. "Then have another cup of tea. I'll be back this evening—with news of Jack, Lord willing."

Can it be true, Lord? Mabel wondered. *Are You behind all this?*

She received no answer, but she drank her second cup of tea more slowly, sunshine from the window soaking into her skin.

*****

The day wore on. Mabel sat in her room, feeling as though she should stay up and wait for news about Jack. But the room was so safe and quiet, and her body so exhausted, that she couldn't help it. She slept through most of the day.

The maidservant woke her again when the sunlight had turned to the rich gold of evening.

"So sorry to wake you, Mrs. Finch," she whispered. "But Mr. Mitchell just got back and said he should speak with you."

Mabel sprang to her feet. She raked a hurried hand through her hair, barely knowing why, then followed the maidservant down to the dining hall at a run.

Percy sat at the same table, this time with a repast of meat, vegetables, potatoes, and gravy before him. Mabel's mouth watered at the sight of the food, but she forced herself to focus on his face instead.

"Jack?" she croaked.

Percy shook his head, his mouth turning down at the corners. He seemed pallid to Mabel; there were dark rings beneath his eyes. "I'm so sorry, Mabel. I enquired after him as far as I could, but found nothing. The workhouse kept a record of selling him to a chimney-sweep. I believe he gave a false name. No one could tell me where he lived."

Mabel sagged. The absence had crushed her like a boulder for a year, yet in that moment, it seemed to grow heavier. She bowed her head, and the rich, savoury scents of the food made her stomach cry out, but her throat closed and tears choked her.

"Please, Mabel, please don't look so sad." Percy laid a gentle hand on her arm. "I know how awful this must be for you, but it isn't over. Jack has to be out there somewhere. We will find him."

Mabel covered her mouth with a hand to hold back a sob. "I'm sorry," she said.

"What do you have to be sorry for?" said Percy.

"You've been so very kind." Mabel hastily dried her eyes. "You must think me ungrateful, but please know that I'm anything but. I just—I need my baby back, Percy."

"And we're going to get him back," said Percy fiercely. "I've already found an investigator on Albury Street. He's apparently very good. He'll help us to find Jack."

Mabel swallowed. "I can't pay him," she whispered.

"You own a farm, my dear," said Percy. "In a few months you will be able to pay anyone you please, and in the meantime, don't worry about it. I'll cover it."

Mabel stared at him. "Why... why would you do such a thing? Why would you do all this?"

Percy's jaw clenched. "Because I should have helped you long ago, Mabel. Helping you now—after six years of suffering I could have saved you from—is the least I could do."

It was difficult to believe that anyone could have intentions so noble, but looking into Percy's eyes, Mabel almost could.

*****

The investigator's office was really just a front room in his home, a Gothic cottage with charming decorative brickwork and a pretty flower garden tended by a smiling young wife who waved them inside.

"Geoffrey's expecting you," she said.

Geoffrey Chancellor was a handsome man, if bearing the evidence that his pretty wife was a good cook as well as a good gardener. The extra curves to his cheeks and belly suited his round face and endearing freckles. Mabel exhaled slightly as he shook Percy's hand; she clung to the lawyer's arm for dear life.

"Mr. Mitchell, please come in," he said. "Tell me how I can help you."

They sat at a narrow desk in a meticulously scrubbed and tidy little office. Mr. Chancellor took out a crisp white notebook and pen, which he filled with ink before raising it above the book.

"Your note said that you were searching for a lost child," he said.

"That's right," said Percy. "My friend, Mrs. Finch, had the great misfortune of ending up in a workhouse for the past year. Her little boy was taken from her there."

"A workhouse, eh?" Mr. Chancellor glanced at Mabel with a hint of distaste in his expression.

"The one in Deptford Creek." Percy pushed a slip of paper to Mr. Chancellor. "This is the name of the chimney sweep who bought him, but I believe it to be fake."

Mr. Chancellor took the paper and frowned at it. "Indeed, indeed." He stroked his smooth chin. "I'm afraid you may be right, Mr. Mitchell. I take pride in knowing most of the folk around here, and I have never seen this name before.

Whoever this Reginald Grimshaw is, I fear he might not be real, or else from a different part of London."

Percy eagerly stepped toward the desk. "Will you be able to help us?" he asked. "Can you find Jack?" He reached into his pocket, and coins clinked.

Mr. Chancellor's eyes glinted. "Of course, Mr. Mitchell, of course," he said. "I'll find the boy quickly, you can be sure of that."

"How quickly?" Mabel asked.

Mr. Chancellor gave her that look again; the distasteful, distrustful one she'd often received from people in the workhouse or on the streets when they saw her in workhouse clothes. "I can't say, ma'am, not knowing where he is. Weeks, perhaps. But I will write often to update you on my progress."

"Weeks," Mabel whispered, strength draining from her limbs at the thought. At the same time, she was hardly surprised. London was a great warren of activity and people and chimney sweeps and little boys named Jack. She could hardly expect any less.

Percy's hand hesitated in his pocket.

"Perhaps less," said Mr. Chancellor quickly, "perhaps more. I really can't say." He spread his hands. "That is why I ask only a moderate weekly fee, and a full reward when the boy is found."

"Of course," said Percy smoothly. He withdrew a small bag of coins from his pocket. "This is a month's fee in advance, Mr. Chancellor."

Mr. Chancellor scooped up the bag in a swift, efficient movement. "Thank you kindly, sir. I will write at once when I find out anything."

Percy took Mabel's arm, and she allowed herself to be steered to the door for a moment before digging in her heels. She looked back at the paunchy figure at his little desk and whispered, "Sir, please... please find my boy."

Mr. Chancellor didn't look up; he was staring into the coin bag.

"I will," he said.

They walked out of the cottage together, Mabel clinging to Percy though she hardly knew why, and nodded at the little wife before turning down the street.

"Don't be afraid, Mabel." Percy laid a hand over hers where it rested on his arm. "He'll find Jack."

"I hope so," Mabel whispered. "I'll pay you back, you know. From the farm."

Percy tilted his head. "Don't worry about that just yet." He paused. "I thought you might want to stay in London."

Stay in London! Mabel longed to do so with all of her heart. She wanted to be as close as possible to her poor little Jack, even if she didn't know where he was.

"I would have liked to," she said quietly, "but I owe him better than that." She squared her shoulders. "I must go back to the farm, Percy. I must make it beautiful and fruitful, and earn a good living, and pay you back, and pay Mr. Chancellor to keep looking until he finds him." Her voice cracked, but she kept talking.

"I must make it wonderful for my little boy so that when we find him and bring him there, he can be safe and happy, with plenty of room to play and a beautiful home to stay in, and everything he needs. I want him to go to school, you know. I want—" Mabel could hardly speak now, and croaked the last words. "I want everything for him."

Percy patted her hand. For several long seconds, he couldn't say a word.

Finally, he said, "Let's get you back to your farm, Mabel," and hailed the next cab.

*****

"We're here," said Percy.

His gentle voice nudged Mabel out of an exhausted doze. She sat up, blushing at the thought she'd fell asleep in the seat opposite him with only the coachman for a chaperone, but then quickly forgot her embarrassment.

The carriage creaked to a halt in front of a run-down farmhouse with creepers covering the front. Beyond, Mabel glimpsed the rooftop that stood in disrepair on top of the old barn, and the fields beyond, pale green in the warmth of early summer.

"Oh," she said softly. "Here we are, then."

She stepped out of the carriage, moving very slowly, and stood in front of the house for a long few minutes.

The coachman stepped down and petted the horses, staring in disapproval at the half-ruined house.

"We could have stopped at your house first, Percy," said Mabel gently.

He shook his head. "I've waited nearly six years for this. I can't wait to see you home again." He pressed a rusty key into her hand. "Welcome home, Mabel."

She drifted to the front door. It was sticky, and she had to wriggle the key to unlock it. The interior was dingy and silent, every surface covered in dust, but everything was exactly as she had left it the day she fled Alf and Ada: the same furniture clustered around the dead fireplace, the same little writing desk by the window, even the same teapot and tray on the coffee table.

"Nothing's been stolen," Mabel marvelled despite the missing tiles that allowed slants of sunlight to turn to golden pools on the floor.

"Of course not," said Percy. "This isn't London."

She remembered being terrified in this place, but with Ned so long gone, the farmhouse had lost its horrors. More than that, Mabel realized. Ned had been harsh and cruel, but he'd left this place to her, not to his sister. Perhaps that was enough to soften his memory a little.

"This is mine," she whispered. She had never owned anything except for her clothes and a few small things before.

"Yes," said Percy. "It's all yours."

It felt impossible even as Mabel led him to the kitchen, where her pots and pans still stood in their cabinets, although mice had nested in several of them. Then she pushed open the back door and they wandered into the barnyard.

The barn was sad and quiet, much of its roof missing, its walls holey and tumbledown. Her cow and horse were long gone; she felt a pang of sorrow at the fate of the poor horse. But beyond that stretched the first paddock, the one where the horse had grazed, and it was knee-deep in fragrant green grass.

"It's in a dreadful state, isn't it?" said Percy.

Mabel turned to him. He stood with his hands in his pockets, head slightly tilted, staring at her. Everything she saw was soft; the curves of his hair, the rumples of his jacket, the expression in his eyes.

"It's all right," she said quietly. "I'm here now. You brought me home, Percy."

Tears glimmered briefly in his eyes before he looked away.

Mabel turned to the paddock and imagined little Jack running in that deep grass, dyed honey gold by the evening sun. She imagined him climbing the tree and running in the barnyard, chasing chickens. She imagined cooking him big, hearty meals in her kitchen, food right from her own garden, grain from their fields.

Mabel spread her arms. "Look at all this grazing! I see Farmer Thornton across the stream has more cattle than ever. I'll hire out the grazing; that'll give us what we need to keep going and to repair the barn and the bits of the house we really need. Then I'll plant vegetables—the seeds are easy to come by—and sell what we don't need. Perhaps it'll be enough to hire another horse by harvest time.

We could plant a winter crop or raise a few pigs, and have enough to plough these fields again in the spring." Her excitement grew as she spoke. "If the harvest is good, we'll be able to finish repairing the house, and perhaps get another dairy cow."

Percy's eyes shone as he gazed at her. "Look at you," he murmured. "Everything you've been through, yet you have so much joy and hope."

Mabel raised her chin. "We will find him, Percy. We *must* find him."

Percy laid a hand on her shoulder. "Of course we will. We'll bring Jack here to enjoy this place, Mabel. You mark my words. We must be faithful and keep praying; the Lord is able to do this, too."

It was difficult, sometimes, to think of God. Polly had made it so much easier to trust Him. But maybe Percy made it easier, too.

Mabel stared across the grassy field and felt sudden peace in her soul. Her son's absence was still a yawning hole in her life, but here, she'd carve out a life for him while Mr. Chancellor searched for him. She'd never thought she'd stand on this acreage knowing she owned, yet here she was.

God was capable of this. She had to trust that He was capable of bringing Jack to her, too.

Chapter Thirteen

Six Months Later

Mabel grunted with effort as she hoisted the last pumpkin from the pile at her garden gate. The huge, glowing orange object dragged on her sore and tired shoulders, but she grinned with triumph as she staggered across the front yard with it in her arms and nudged open the freshly painted gate.

"Mabel!" Percy hurried over. "Let me take that for you."

"It's quite all right, Percy, thank you." Mabel heaved the pumpkin into the back of the carriage, then stepped back, arms akimbo, to survey her handiwork. Both carriage seats and the space in between were piled high with enormous fat pumpkins. Not a mark lay on any of them; Mabel had ensured that no insects or diseases came near them.

"They're beautiful," said Percy.

"Thank you." Mabel blushed. "And thank you for letting me load the pumpkins into your carriage. I could really have hired a wagon or made a few trips with the wheelbarrow."

"Not at all. The livery in town charges ridiculous prices, and I know Farmer Thornton is particularly stingy. It would have been silly to pay those prices when we could use my perfectly good carriage," said Percy. "Come on, let's get to the market. We want to sell these before the horse sale begins."

Mabel clambered onto the front seat and took the reins; Percy hadn't driven himself much. She slapped them lightly on his bay carriage horse's back and the animal set off with a grunt of surprise at the sudden weight behind it. It plodded along, toiling under the weight, but the short journey to the village didn't take long.

The marketplace bustled. Stalls stood all over the cobbled yard, with rosy-cheeked farmers and their wives selling barrels of apples, sacks of corn and barley, and bags of soil-streaked potatoes. A fiddler stood on the corner, coaxing a merry tune from his elderly instrument with his cap on the ground at his feet.

Once they'd unloaded the pumpkins around a large table, Percy sat down to write "Pumpkins" and their price on a slate. Mabel wandered over to the fiddler and fished for her purse. She lifted a precious penny and tossed it into his cap.

"Cor, miss," said the fiddler. "Thank you!"

Mabel smiled and returned to the stall.

"I'll take him a shilling later," said Percy, "but now I think we have our first customers."

He beamed as a young couple approached the table, the husband waving a bag of coins.

"We've been watching your pumpkins over the fence all autumn, Mabel," he said. "We were hoping you'd bring them to market."

"I'll take three," said the wife.

The husband stacked them on top of each other and carried them away while the wife paid Mabel. She still couldn't help admiring the flash of sunlight on copper as she slipped the coins into her apron pocket. She glanced at the straw bales set up in the centre of the square—the auction ring—and her heart bumped against her ribs in excitement.

Percy followed her gaze and smiled. "It's a big day for you."

"Maybe," said Mabel. "Maybe. The pumpkins have to do well first."

*****

The pumpkins did well. Better than well. Farmer Hoggart had tried growing them too, but the slugs had left them patterned with their trails, and they couldn't compare to the healthy orange of Mabel's. People flocked to her table. Many judged her; others demanded when she would get remarried; yet others eyed the pumpkins, then Percy, then her with great suspicion.

She only had two left when the church bell struck eleven and a whiskery old farmer ambled up to the stall.

"Expensive, for pumpkins," he grunted.

Mabel smiled sweetly. "Farmer Hoggart is selling them, too. I believe his price is lower."

The whiskery farmer, Farmer James, eyed the marred offerings on Hoggart's table and shuddered. "Never mind. I'll take both."

"Let me take them to your wagon for you, sir," said Percy.

"What are you doing here with this?" the farmer demanded. "Aren't you an attorney?"

"Indeed, sir, but it's Saturday and I spent my weekends as I please." Percy gave her a sparkling look and carried the pumpkins away with quick, sure strides.

Farmer James sighed as he handed over the money. "When are you selling?" he asked.

Mabel had heard the question often enough, but as always, it made her bristle. She took his money and met his eyes. "I beg your pardon?"

"The farm, woman," said Farmer James. "When are you selling the farm?"

Mabel raised her chin. "It's not for sale," she said coolly.

"It's not natural," Farmer James hissed. "A woman on her own on a place like that."

Mabel gestured at her empty table. "My pumpkins aren't protesting, sir."

"Insolent wench!" said Farmer James, and stormed off.

Percy returned, almost bumping into him. As the lanky lawyer strode towards her, soft hair bouncing over his forehead, the thought flitted across Mabel's mind that perhaps she wouldn't be alone forever.

She pushed it aside, blushing.

"What's gotten into him?" Percy asked.

"Oh, never mind him," said Mabel, excitedly counting her day's money. "Am I doing the arithmetic right? Is it— is it enough?"

Percy beamed. "Together with the money you took out of the bank from Farmer Thornton's grazing hire, it's more than enough, Mae."

She loved the nickname, but she didn't know how to tell him so.

"Come on," said Percy, grasping her arm. "They're starting!"

He hustled her to the ring of straw bales as a boy strode inside, wrestling with a cantankerous little colt who kept rearing and trying to bite. An auctioneer in a cloth cap chuckled at the sight.

"Now then, gentlemen," he said, "here's a fine youngster for you. Strong, isn't he? Opening bid starting at five pounds."

The second lot was the one Mabel wanted. She wrung her hands as the colt sold for fifteen pounds. It seemed an absurd amount of money even to think of; yet more absurd was the fact that she had more than that amount in her apron pocket at that moment, thanks to the farm.

She glanced at Percy. *Thanks to Percy*, she corrected herself.

"Lot two now, gentlemen," said the auctioneer. "A strapping seven-year-old cob mare. Good to drive and ride."

Mabel held her breath as the mare came into the ring. She plodded patiently beside the boy leading her, familiar from her flaxen mane to her wide white blaze, the carbon copy of the horse that was killed in the accident. She would be; she was his half sister. Mabel had seen her in the fields of the breeder where Ned had bought the poor gelding.

"Starting at ten pounds," said the auctioneer.

Immediately, several farmers started bidding. Eleven pounds. Twelve. Mabel's heart thudded as she raised her hand, and the auctioneer stared at her for a beat, startled to see a woman standing in the crowd. Then Percy edged nearer to her, and the auctioneer went on.

"Thirteen pounds from the, ah, the lady. Fourteen pounds, thank you, sir. Fifteen..."

The bids rose. Mabel bid again at seventeen, then again at twenty. Finally, the bids trickled down at twenty-two, and the crowd started to shake their heads and look away. The last farmer who'd bid grinned smugly.

"Go on, Mae," said Percy softly.

"Going once," said the auctioneer. "Going twice..."

Mabel raised her hand. "Twenty-three pounds."

The auctioneer didn't hesitate this time. "Twenty-three pounds I'm bid. Twenty-three for the lovely cob mare. Look at those legs and head, gentlemen! Twenty-three pounds. Twenty-four, sir? Twenty-four?"

The farmer shook his head.

"Going once, going twice, sold to the lady." The auctioneer nodded to her.

"Well done, Mae." Percy beamed. "She's all yours."

"Can you believe it?" Mabel cried, happy tears stinging her eyes. "Oh, Percy, this will make so many things possible for us. We can cut hay in the meadow and sell it instead of hiring the land to stingy old Farmer Thornton. We can plough and plant the fields next year. We'll have an even greater harvest next autumn, and maybe sweet Jack can learn to ride on her." The thought of her son made her throat tighten.

"Maybe Mr. Chancellor will have something when I go to London next week," said Percy.

"I hope so," said Mabel softly. "I really do…" She sighed. "You know, I have the perfect name for my new horse."

"Oh?" said Percy. "What is it?"

Mabel smiled. "Polly." She had to clear her throat before she could continue. "I'll name her Polly."

"It's a good name," said Percy.

"I miss her every day, you know," said Mabel quietly. "You would have loved her. She was so much like you."

Percy hesitated. "Would you like to pay your respects to her?"

"You mean, at her grave?" Mabel asked.

"That's right."

"Oh, I don't know. It's close to Charlie's house. I'd have to pass right by it…" The thought of laying flowers on Polly's grave nonetheless brought tears to her eyes.

"I'll go with you," said Percy.

"Percy, that would be so kind," Mabel whispered. "I don't know…"

"I'll go with you," said Percy again. "You can join me on the trip to London next week. We'll only be gone a few days; I'm sure my housekeeper won't mind feeding your chickens. It's a nice walk."

"Oh, Percy, thank you." Mabel smiled. "Do you know what?"

"What?"

"We can take my horse," said Mabel, laughing.

*****

Mabel clutched the bunch of flowers in both hands as she sat in Percy's carriage, admiring the gleaming haunches of her mare Polly as the patient little cob pulled the carriage through London. The cob's ears twitched at all the new sounds, but she'd been admirable so far, according to the coachman.

"I'm so pleased about the news," said Percy, sitting across from her.

"Me too." Mabel grinned. "If Mr. Chancellor's finally found the sweep who bought Jack, I'm sure it won't be long before he finds Jack himself."

"Soon you'll have your little boy in your arms again," said Percy gently.

Mabel sighed. "I pray so."

She gazed out of the window, and a jolt ran through her as she recognized the street where she'd birthed Jack in what felt like a lifetime ago.

"What is it?" Percy asked.

"We're close," Mabel croaked. "We're very close to Charlie's cottage."

Percy laid a hand on her knee. "He won't know it's you. I'll draw the curtains."

"No, there's no need. It's all right." Mabel edged close to the window and opened it. "I'd like to see the cottage one more time."

Percy sat in respectful silence as they drove past the smithy and its tiny cottage, which looked very different, like a lantern with the light blown out and cobwebs in the corners and dust on the wick. Polly's absence was written loud in the lack of flowers and the dusty windowpanes. Even the anvil was silent. Mabel wondered if Charlie still lived there at all.

"It's sad to see it like this," she murmured.

Only a few minutes later, they stopped at the only cemetery where Charlie would conceivably have buried Polly. It was the closest to the cottage by several miles, the gravestones clustered at the feet of the same little church where Mabel was supposed to have married him. Percy walked with her as she disembarked from the carriage and moved among the sad little stones. Many were rough-hewn; several graves were marked only with little cairns or anonymous wooden crosses.

She feared she would never find Polly's grave, but finally, she did. It stood in the shadow of a hedge, tucked close to the church's foundations, and the simple gravestone read only *Polly Wilson.*

"Oh, Polly," Mabel whispered. She crouched and laid her flowers on the grave. "I'm so sorry."

She blinked rapidly, wondering what Polly would think of her now. Polly would have loved the farm. But she would have been utterly heartbroken to know what had happened to Jack. And what would she have thought of Charlie and Mabel being apart?

Look after him, if he lets you. They'd been among Polly's last words.

"Mabel?"

"Excuse me, sir," said Percy firmly, "I'd rather you didn't—"

"Mabel, is it really you?"

Mabel thought her mind was playing tricks on her, but when she spun around, it really was him. It was Charlie. He stood there in the flesh, his hair still the colour of straw despite the odd streak of grey, his cheeks still red, his eyes still gentle despite the dark rings underneath them.

"Oh, Mabel," he said. "I've finally found you!"

Percy stepped between them. "Sir—" he began.

"It's all right, Percy," Mabel blurted out. "Let him—let him."

Percy glanced at her, and she saw something shatter in his expression. Then he stepped back and Charlie rushed up to her. He seized her hands in grimy, hard fingers and stared at her like she was the rising sun, like a man in a desert finally coming across a crisp, clear stream.

"Oh, Mabel!" he whispered. "Where have you been?"

Mabel stiffened. "In the workhouse, Charlie."

His face fell.

"Where did you think I would go when you told me to leave?" she said.

Charlie's face crumpled. "I'm so sorry. I should never have said that... I should never have said any of those awful, terrible things that I told you that night." Tears spilled down his cheeks. "You know what Polly meant to me, Mabel. You know... you know how much I loved her." His hands tightened. "But I never stopped loving you. I said awful things—stupid, stupid, awful things—but I didn't mean them."

Mabel searched his face, trying to believe him.

"They took Jack from me," she said, her voice breaking. "They took him away from me in the workhouse, Charlie, and I've been searching for him for six months."

"It's my fault, I know it is," Charlie cried. "I'm sorry. I'm so, so sorry, Mabel. Please, you have to believe me. Please—" He stopped, staring at the ring. "You... you're still wearing your ring."

Mabel glanced at the iron band encircling her left ring finger. "Yes," she whispered.

Charlie took a deep breath, as if to compose himself. "Then maybe I still have a chance," he said, and sank to his knees.

"Charlie—" Mabel began.

"I'm begging your forgiveness, Mabel." He searched her eyes. "Please, with everything in me, I'm begging you. I don't deserve all the good you are. If you turn away now, I'll understand why. But if you ever loved me, give me another chance. I can be better. I can do better. I'll help you find Jack. We can do that together…"

Mabel looked helplessly toward Percy, but he was gone; she saw his silhouette by the carriage hitched to her horse. Guilt surged through her, but then the horse's name flitted through her mind.

Polly.

She'd promised Polly she would care for Charlie if he let her. She'd thought that he wouldn't, but now…

"I have a farm," she blurted out.

"What?" Charlie frowned, puzzled.

"Ned left me the farm after all," said Mabel. "It's outside London. I… I do quite well there." She cleared her throat. "The village smith is getting old, too. Perhaps he'll want an apprentice."

Charlie's face glowed with joy. "Are you saying yes?" he said. "Will you still marry me?"

The thought of marrying him made her balk, but she pushed it aside. "Let's just get the hay in first," she said.

Charlie leaped to his feet and gripped her hands. "Oh, Mabel, Mabel!" he cried. "Praise God that I found you again!"

His laughter still sounded like music, and Mabel couldn't help but giggle when he picked her up and swung her around and around.

*****

The carriage seemed almost too small for the three of them, but perhaps that was because of the silence that hung in the carriage like a chain curtain. Charlie sat beside Mabel with his hand on her knee. Percy sat opposite, alone, staring out of the carriage window. He had hardly said a word since the cemetery, where he'd offered his congratulations to Charlie and Mabel with a smile that seemed like a great effort.

Now, the hills of home rolled all around them, and soon the village's church spire came into view.

"There," said Mabel. "That's our village."

Charlie brightened, squeezing her knee. "*Our* village. I like the sound of that."

Percy swallowed, his Adam's apple bobbing.

Polly whinnied as they trotted down their lane.

"She knows where her stable is," said Mabel, laughing.

"Good old Polly," said Charlie affectionately.

The carriage rattled to a halt, and Charlie leaped out. "Good heavens, Mabel!" he cried. "Is that our house?"

"That will be our house, yes." Mabel stepped out, smiling. "Isn't it beautiful?"

It *was* beautiful again now, with the wisteria she'd planted climbing the facade and the newly whitewashed window frames glowing in the setting sunlight. Charlie gaped at it, open-mouthed.

"Go on." Mabel gave him the key. "Have a look around before Percy's coachman takes you up to the inn to get settled."

Charlie grinned like a little boy as he took the key and bounded into the house, and finally, at last, Mabel and Percy were alone for a moment.

She turned to him. "Percy—"

"Please." Percy smiled despite the sorrow in his eyes. "Don't apologize or thank me. This is everything you deserve, Mabel."

"You've been wonderful, you know," she said.

"So have you," said Percy, and his voice held the same kindness as always.

The thought that she was making a terrible mistake flitted through Mabel's mind.

"I've given Mr. Chancellor your address," said Percy awkwardly. "He'll write to you when he has a new lead on Jack."

Mabel nodded. She'd been paying Mr. Chancellor herself for several months now, and Charlie could read the letters to her. The sinking sensation in her stomach came from the sense she had that Percy was saying goodbye.

And why wouldn't he?

"Percy, you've been better to us than—than I deserve," she managed.

Percy forced a smile. "I don't think so," he said quietly. "I believe all I've done is repay what I owed you." He took her hand and kissed it delicately, the most exquisite sensation she'd ever experienced. "Goodbye, Mae."

He got into the carriage then, and Charlie was calling her from inside the house.

So she turned and went to him.

*****

The next weeks of gathering a last cutting of hay passed far too quickly.

The work itself was effortless. With Polly pulling the mower, cutting it went swiftly, and with the precious sunshine beating on Mabel's shoulders and the smell of cut grass rising in her nostrils, it was beautiful. It gave her far too much time to think, though, to constantly wonder if she was doing the right thing.

If Charlie was the right thing.

He worked as an apprentice at the smithy, but every afternoon he came by to visit her when Anna—who'd returned to her service with a broad smile—was working in the garden and Mabel was cooking. He'd stand in the kitchen and drink a cup of tea, listening while she talked and talked about the farm. Anything to keep him from talking about the wedding.

Sometimes, she thought she smelled a little something on his breath. She always dismissed it. It was the bad memories from Ned's time that did it, she thought. Charlie had never.

Charlie would never.

*****

With one of Charlie Thornton's farm hands pitching forkfuls of hay onto the wagon and Polly pulling, they gathered the hay just in time.

The first raindrops began to fall when Mabel ran into the house, leaving the horse tucked up in the barn with ample hay. She darted into the sanctuary of her clean, well-stocked kitchen and put the kettle on, knowing Charlie would be here soon. Anna was in the sanctuary of the garden shed nearby, planting seedling trays.

Maybe he won't come in the rain, she thought, and pushed the uncharitable hope away. He was the man she was going to marry—for Polly's sake. She'd promised she would take care of him if he let her. She knew Polly would love to see Charlie here on this beautiful farm, living a new life.

Mabel had loved him once. He was good and gentle; he wouldn't hurt her like Ned had done. That had to be good enough for her.

She crushed the silly thoughts and poured tea into the pot. As another fat raindrop pinged off the roof, she heard the distant, cheerful whistle from the lane; Charlie.

He always had a merry tune on his lips, and Mabel smiled. She'd always loved that about him.

It wouldn't be so bad, having that happy whistle around the house. Far better than Ned's yelling, in any case.

She strode to the front door and opened it in the drizzle as Charlie ambled down the road toward her. At first, she tried to ignore the warning bell ringing in the back of her mind as Charlie approached. There was something funny about his walk—a little weave, a slight unsteadiness.

Don't be ridiculous, Mabel, she chided herself.

"Hello, my love!" Charlie sang. "Hello, my pretty one!"

Mabel's intestines tied themselves in a knot. She froze when he reached her and leaned in to kiss her cheek, as he always did, and a terrible wave of breath rolled over her. The smell was despicably familiar, completely unmistakable.

Mabel lunged back. "Charlie, what have you been doing?" she demanded.

"Working for the smith, dear," said Charlie, swaggering into the house. He fell onto the sofa and put his feet up on the armrest despite the mud on his boots.

Anger curdled in Mabel's belly. She folded her arms and stood over him. "Have you been drinking?"

"I just wet my whistle a little, dear. To celebrate the hay," said Charlie.

Mabel shivered. At least he wasn't belligerent, like Ned was when he was drunk. She could live with this. She reminded herself that she had lived with much worse.

"What's the matter?" asked Charlie.

Mabel sighed and thought of Polly. "Nothing," she murmured. "Nothing at all."

Her thoughts raced as she went to the kitchen and made the tea. Charlie had never touched a drop when she'd lived with him and Polly, but then again... that was before Polly died.

She returned to find Charlie with his hands behind his head, gazing blissfully at the ceiling as he whistled between his teeth.

"Here's your tea," she said.

"You know," Charlie slurred, "when I saw you in the carriage, I never dreamed you had a farm. I dreamed of a lot of things, but never a farm."

Mabel frowned. "You saw me in the carriage?"

"Of course." Charlie laughed. "How d'you think I followed you to the cemetery?"

Goosebumps prickled on Mabel's neck. She lowered the tea tray to the coffee table, watching him. "I thought..." She swallowed. "I thought it was a miracle. An act of God."

"I was sitting in the cottage," Charlie slurred. "Finally begged a few pennies for a beer... last beer, of course. And then I saw you go by. And I thought to myself, now that Mabel, she was always a hard worker."

Mabel stared at him. "*Begged*? Charlie, what are you talking about?"

Charlie waved a sloppy hand, almost knocking over the tea.

"You had an excellent job, Charlie. Better than all of us. You should have had more than enough without any extra mouths to feed," Mabel protested.

"Oh, you know. The old smith's still alive, the tough old blighter. Never did die," said Charlie, "and then there was all that trouble with the nail-bound horses…"

"You'd never nail-bind a horse," said Mabel sharply. Then she paused. "Not if you were sober."

"Eh." Charlie shrugged.

Mabel sank onto the chair opposite him. "Charlie, when did you start drinking?"

He heard the edge in her tone and sat up suddenly. "It doesn't matter, Mabel." He reached across the coffee table. "All that matters is I'm here with you now."

Mabel pulled her hands away from him. "Charlie."

He glared.

"Was it after Polly died?" she demanded.

"How can you be so heartless, Mabel?" he cried. "Of course it was after Polly died."

The pieces slowly came together in Mabel's mind. "You said… you said you begged pennies for a last beer. Were you going to stop?"

He barked a laugh with the uninhibited honesty of alcohol. "No. It was my last beer at—" He stopped.

She held his gaze. "Tell me the truth, Charlie."

"It doesn't matter." He tried a sloppy grin. "It all worked out for—"

"Don't you dare." Mabel rose to her feet. "Don't implicate God in what—what I'm starting to believe was nothing but a scheme."

Charlie's eyes narrowed. "Scheme? What do you take me for?"

"You said you saw me go past and you knew I was a hard worker." Mabel balled her hands into fists. "You had a thousand chances to save me from the workhouse. It was only a few blocks from the cottage. It would have been easy to guess that I was there. You could have asked, Charlie. You could have saved me. But instead, you only grew interested in me when you saw me well-dressed and riding in a carriage. Then you followed me to the cemetery."

Charlie's jaw clenched, but he said nothing.

"You didn't come to me for love," said Mabel, more softly now. "You came to me because you'd lost everything, hadn't you? You started drinking when Polly died and you couldn't stop. Then you were leaving horses nail-bound—lame—and the smith was refusing to give you any work. He was going to kick you out of the cottage, wasn't he?"

"He had a new apprentice," Charlie snarled. "He wanted me gone by the end of the month."

Mabel shook her head. "I can't believe this. I can't believe you."

"What does it matter why I went up to you the first time? I do love you," said Charlie.

"Oh, so you admit it," said Mabel.

Charlie sneered.

Mabel stared at him, smelled his breath, thought of Jack. How could she do this to him? She couldn't bring him home to her beautiful farm and a drunkard stepfather. She'd lived under Ned's thumb for too long to believe that being with a drunkard would be the right life for her boy.

Look after him, if he lets you, Polly had said. She'd understood Charlie's weakness.

She'd given Mabel permission to do what she had to do to protect Jack and herself. Tears filled her eyes at the thought of this last act of love from Polly, and that was what made up her mind.

"Get out," she said softly.

Charlie rose. "I beg your pardon?"

"You heard me," said Mabel. "Leave my house at once."

"How dare you speak to me like that, woman!" Charlie raged.

He didn't raise a hand, but his voice made her cringe. It echoed through the years the way Ned's voice had echoed, filled with unreasonable rage, with the fury of one who'd wronged her and then blamed her for it.

Something flared within. It was a strength beyond her own understanding, a sudden peace that left no room for cowering. Perhaps it was the same thing by which Polly had gone with such calm courage to her death and the pearly gates for which she'd longed all her life.

Mabel raised her head.

"This is my house," she said. "I want you to leave."

Charlie raised a hand then, but Mabel stepped nearer to him, and they were nose to nose.

"Charlie," she said, "you have to go now." She pulled off the ring and thrust it into his breast pocket. "Goodbye."

He stared at her, and then Anna said from the kitchen, "I'd listen to her if I were you."

For once, Mabel was glad of her ever-nosy friend. Charlie glanced from Anna to Mabel, reading in their eyes the strength of two women who'd farmed this land alone all summer.

"Polly would be ashamed of you," he hissed.

Mabel smiled. "Polly rests in paradise, and I'll love her always."

When even this jab made no difference, Charlie realized he was beaten. He gave her a last, sullen glare, then shoved through the door and disappeared into the rainy night.

"And good riddance, too," said Anna. "I never did like him. Now you can go to Percy."

Mabel turned to her, wide-eyed. "Wh-what?"

"You two have been in love all this time, dear," said Anna. "Didn't you see? He loved you better than anything. How could you not know?"

Mabel's heart pounded hard. "But... but after what I did to him... how can I go to him now?"

Anna smiled. "By faith, my dear," she said.

Sudden certainty flooded Mabel's veins. Her blood pounded in her, hard and fierce.

"I have to go to him," she cried, rushing to the kitchen.

"What?" said Anna.

"I have to go to him right now!" said Mabel. "Anna, keep the fire going. I'll be back!"

Then she ran to the barn in the rain, saddled Polly with shaking hands, and pulled herself onto the good mare's back. As the rain drummed on her bonnet, she whirled Polly onto the lane and kicked her into a gallop.

*****

Mabel was no great rider, but she was mounted on a wonderful horse. Dear Polly didn't put a foot wrong as she splashed through the puddles, galloped down the lane, and clattered across the market square. They turned to Percy's house, and for a wild moment, Mabel feared he wasn't in. Then she saw the golden light in his windows shimmering through the rain and she knew that this was her chance.

She pulled Polly up in front of the door, wrapped her reins around the fence rail, and ran to the front door. There, her courage almost forsook her. She stood, trembling, in the rain for a few moments.

Lord, help me, she prayed.

Then she found the courage to knock, hammering harder than she'd meant thanks to the rain that made her hands tremble.

Don't let it be the housekeeper, she hoped silently. *Let it be him! Let it—*

The door swung open, and there he was. Percy. Softness in every line of his smile, the look in his eyes, the curves of his hair. He wore a pinstriped suit, but his tie was loosened, and there were slippers on his feet.

His eyes widened. "Mae? Are you all right?"

"Better than I've ever been," Mabel cried truthfully over the thundering rain.

"You'd better come in," said Percy.

"No. This can't wait." Mabel squared her shoulders. "Percy, I came here to apologize."

He stared at her. "You don't owe me that, Mae."

"Yes, I do," said Mabel. "I—" She spotted a suitcase in the hall. "Where are you going?"

He looked away. "London," he said. "For good, this time."

She swallowed hard. "Wh-what?"

"It's for the best, you see," said Percy. "I couldn't stay here. Not…" He shook his head. "It doesn't matter. How can I help you?"

"Oh, Percy," said Mabel softly, understanding that he was leaving because of her. "You've already helped me more than enough. More than anyone has ever done."

He stared at her.

"I should have seen that earlier. I should have known," she whispered.

"It's all right. There's no need for that," said Percy.

"There is a need to tell you this, though." Mabel swallowed hard. "I want you to stay."

He froze. "But Charlie…"

"I told him to leave," said Mabel. "I hope to never see him again."

Percy gaped at her.

"He only wanted to take advantage of what I have. He doesn't love me," said Mabel, "and I have had enough of men who don't know how to love."

Her heart bounded as a long silence stretched between them, underlined by the steady drizzle.

"Mae," Percy whispered.

He crossed the distance between them in one stride and cupped her wet face in his hands. Rain coursed between his fingers and dripped on his hair. He didn't seem to care.

"I love you, Mae," he gushed. "I've always loved you. Will you—"

"Yes!" said Mabel, laughing. "Yes, yes, yes!"

Epilogue

Rice fell over Mabel's head like snow, scattering on her shoulders, mingling with the flowers in her braided hair. It settled on the shoulders of her brand new dress, the sky-blue one she'd spent so many hours making, and on the dark hair of the bridegroom by her side.

Percy's eyes shone. Like Mabel, he wore a real silver wedding band; she felt its smoothness against her fingers where they interlocked with his.

The cheering group of friends and family lining the church steps hurled more rice. Mabel laughed as it showered around her, filling her world with celebration.

At the bottom of the steps, Percy stopped and turned to face her. The mischievous new twinkle in his eye sent a thrill of excitement and anticipation down to Mabel's toes. He wrapped his arms around her and dipped her slightly backwards, then kissed her again, and the crowd cheered.

Percy's coachman, all grins, wearing a rose in his buttonhole, waited in front of the little village church.

Polly had flowers in her mane and someone had oiled her hooves. She stood with her head high, as though understanding the pride and joy of the occasion.

The coachman opened the carriage door and bowed as though they were royalty. Mabel gave a dizzy laugh as Percy scooped her into his arms and lifted her into the carriage, to cheering from the crowd.

He shut the door, muffling the cheers, and the coachman snapped the whip in the air. Polly set off at a bold trot, throwing her hooves high like a hackney, and the set off toward the farmhouse—their home.

Percy kissed her again in the carriage, longer this time. Mabel wrapped her arms around his neck and returned the kiss.

"I love you," she burst out when it ended.

Percy pressed his forehead against hers. "Oh, Mabel. I love you, too."

She sighed with contentment. "I know."

The giddy joy of the ceremony slowly ebbed away, and a familiar weight returned. It was like an old injury that never stopped hurting, but to which she had grown accustomed.

Percy's dark eyes searched hers. "You're thinking of Jack."

"I'm sorry," said Mabel. "I don't want to spoil such a beautiful day."

Percy took her hand and stroked it gently. "Don't apologize, Mae. I wish he were here, too. But next week, we'll go back to London, and this time I'll visit Chancellor myself and have some words with him. Maybe it's time for a new investigator."

"Thank you, Percy." Mabel smiled. "We don't have to talk about it right now. I know that he's in the Lord's hands, wherever he is. We'll keep trying to find him."

"We will find him," said Percy. "I'll do everything in my power."

"I know you will." Mabel beamed. "You always keep your promises."

With that, she laid down her little boy in the arms of the Saviour Who had done so many miracles for her already, and she kissed her new husband with joyful abandon.

It would be alright, she knew it would. God had not brought her this far to abandon her now. As the sun broke through the clouds, a renewed sense of hope filled Mabel's heart. With Percy by her side, their love and faith would guide them to finding Jack, no matter how long the journey took.

The End

Would you like a FREE Book?

Join Iris Coles Newsletter

Would you like a FREE Book?

List of Books

The Stone Picker's Christmas Promise

The Little One's Christmas Dream

The Waif's Lost Family

The Pickpocket Orphans

The Workhouse Girls Despair

The Forgotten Match Girl's Christmas Birthday

The Wretched Needle Worker

The Lost Daughter

The Christmas Pauper